CW01239654

Other works by Hannah-Freya Blake

Poetry

'Transforming Trumpery' in *All is Flux*, edited by M. B. Gerlach, J. L. Rushworth and J. M. Young (Indigo Dreams Publishing, 2020)

'A Goodnight Kiss' in *Stories from Home*, edited by H. Barclay and S. Hehir (Gamoran Publishing, 2020)

'Bitch' in *Confessions*, edited by M. Lofthouse, A. Wilkinson and O. Hardwick (Indigo Dreams Publishing, 2022)

'Burning' in *Sleeping in Frozen Quiet*, edited by H. Blake and E. Stockdale (Indigo Dreams Publishing, 2023)

Short stories

'Murder Manifesto' in *All is Flux*, edited by M. B. Gerlach, J. L. Rushworth and J. M. Young (Indigo Dreams Publishing, 2020)

'A Pocket' in *Stories from Home*, edited by H. Barclay and S. Hehir (Gamoran Publishing, 2020)

Cake Craft

By Hannah-Freya Blake

This is a work of fiction. Names, characters, places, and incidents either are the product of the author's imagination or are used fictitiously. Any resemblance to actual persons, living or dead, events, or locales is entirely coincidental.

Copyright © 2023 by Hannah-Freya Blake

All rights reserved. No part of this book may be reproduced or used in any manner without written permission of the copyright owner except for the use of quotations in a book review.

Cover art & back cover illustration by Mia Carnevale
Editing by Celine Frohn
Back cover design by Charlie Bramald

ISBN 978-1-9163669-7-8 (paperback)
ISBN 978-1-9163669-8-5 (ebook)

Published by Nyx Publishing 2023
Sheffield, United Kingdom
www.nyxpublishing.com

To my maternal grandmother, Nanny.
I know you're excited for me.
Remember: this is a work of fiction!

To my paternal grandmother, Grandma, who would definitely not like the language.
I know you'd still be proud of me.

And to those who have struggled to love themselves.
You are not alone. You are enough.

Contents

Cake Craft	1
Mother Magpie	109
House Proud	120
Old Jack	129
Acknowledgements	143
About the author	145

Cake Craft

1

I used to know the Devil, only back then he was called Arthur, and he was a seventy-eight-year-old dairy farmer from Yorkshire. I was seventeen at the time, in my first job at a nursing home in Keighley. Biscuit bitch, is what my older sister called me, which only tells you half the job: the rest was tea, and washing up, and dashing about the place in search of help when one of the inmates made a run for the door. That's what we called the old folk, the inmates. The home was run just like a prison, too. Early mornings, early bedtimes, with maximum security on the top floor for the doddering escapologists.

That's where Arthur, the Devil, lived. Third floor, M. Hopkins Corridor, Room 9, at the very end. He was tall and stooped and always wore a flat cap. Most days you could hear him bellow down the corridors, raising hell, demanding to know who had taken his hat. I still remember the delight in his eyes whenever I picked up his wrist and dropped it on top of his head, so he could feel that he was still wearing it. *Magic, is that,* he'd tell me with a wink, and then he'd settle into his armchair and promptly fall asleep until it was time for tea.

I didn't make any friends while I was there. Most of the

nurses were too busy, and the other "biscuit bitches" smoked together on their breaks, and my one attempt at going twos made me sick. I threw up on Sarah's new shoes; Sarah played rugby on the weekends and looked like it. I didn't want to piss her off again, so I kept to myself after that.

The inmates twittered a lot, but seldom made much sense. Granny Grace, who always wore these bilious skirts that swallowed up half her little body, would wake up from a nap with a sudden declaration that: *Eeh by gum, there's nowt so queer as folk*. She was one of the easier ones, and her son would visit on weekends with a box of chocolates he'd share with us. Madame Maureen, one of the younger inmates, would swan about the lounge on her tiptoes as if she were in stilettos, but she never said a word to "the help". It was only Arthur I ever had something like a chat with, even if most of that chat was about the whereabouts of his flat cap, or what biscuit I was offering that day with his afternoon brew. It usually went something like this:

"Digestives today, Arthur."

"Don't like digestives."

Or: "Custard creams today, Arthur."

"Don't like custard creams."

And: "Fox's Viennese, Arthur. They're local."

"Don't like Fox's."

He always ate them, even so, and smiled all the while, which was just about the only time he ever did. His smile was kind of creepy though; you could see all his teeth, small and neat, but there seemed to be too many for his mouth. With his thin lips, too, it was like his jaw was trying to sneer through the skin. A grinning skull in a flat cap.

It's been about fifteen years since I worked there—fifteen years since I last saw Arthur. I assume he's dead now. Strange, how memories bubble up, out of nowhere. But it's the biscuits that've done it. I've scoffed my way through a packet of chocolate-covered digestives and decided, on my last bite, that I don't actually like them. I know ice cream is supposed to be the quintessential break-up binge, but I wasn't exactly thinking straight when I went up the road to the supermarket. I came out with a bag of giant marshmallows, Monster Munch, a six pack of fruit cider, and biscuits. Bridget Jones, eat your fucking heart out: this is how we do it up in Yorkshire. And there'll be no Céline Dion, thank you very much. I've gone old school. Soft Cell, "Tainted Love".

I've already done the ritual baking of grandma's parkin. I've done that since my first boyfriend kissed some other girl on a park bench when I was fifteen. Jenny, I think it was. I found her sitting on his lap, snogging him like his face was made of chips and curry sauce or something—all lapping tongue and chomping mouth—while his hands rummaged under her school shirt, on the hunt for something to squeeze to death. I ran off before they realised I had found them, but I was too ashamed and confused to go home, so I wandered further down the street. Jenny's older brother used to buy us Russian Standard from the corner shop and, sure enough, I found him smoking spliffs with his mate outside A. K. News. I asked him if he'd buy me a bottle. He asked if I had money, and I told him no. He said he'd get me a bottle if I gave him a hand job. He was joking, and his mate thought it was hilarious, in that wheezy, half-choked way stoners laugh. But I said yes and so he bought me a bottle of vodka and then I gave him a hand job behind the bins while his mate stood on watch.

When I got home, I washed my hands and whipped up a parkin batter, mostly to sober up. My sister was away on some school trip, and my mum was on nights, so I had the kitchen to myself, which was just as well—I didn't want any questions. I just wanted to bake, even if only the top oven worked and I had to light the gas hob with a matchstick and burnt my fingers in the process. With the bitter taste of betrayal and the heat of vodka and the sour flavour of Jenny's brother's smoky breath on my tongue, I whisked the batter in diligent silence. I sat on the cold tiled floor for an hour, watching it bake in silence. I ate the whole thing, straight from the tin with a fork, as soon as it stopped burning by tongue. I ate until I felt full and kept eating until I felt sick and I ate until it was all gone.

I bake parkin after every break-up now. I know the recipe by heart. I like to think my grandma would approve. I eat the cake, as if I'm eating my ex, and poof: he's gone. Usually does the trick, but not this time. Cake won't cut it for a divorce a year down the line. Well, we aren't officially divorced just yet. He's been hoping for a promotion at work and reckoned a divorce would scupper his chances, since his new girlfriend is a student of his. Fool that I am I kept playing happy wife for months after, working in his lab and attending functions on his arm. Still hasn't got the fucking promotion, which would delight me if it weren't for the fact that I still don't have the divorce.

I turn up the music to drown out the sound of the neighbours going at it from the flat above, pretending that I don't hear Ollie from downstairs hammering the ceiling to tell me to turn it back down.

2

I wake up on the couch, my hair sticky with cider, my phone buzzing under my arm. Eventually the caller gives up and sends a message instead. I'm tempted to ignore it but I still hope, stupidly, it might be from David. A message to say that finally, after a year, he's realised the younger model doesn't have the right steerage—she's good only for quiet country roads in the summer when you can take the top off, whereas I'm a steady and reliable drive. Much more practical.

It's from my sister: *Turn on Look North x*. I run my hands around the crevices of the couch in search of the remote, clawing up crumbs in my fingernails. Ah, there it is.

Something about a big drug bust in one of those estates my mum used to say we couldn't go, not that ours had been much better growing up. I mute my television, ignoring it—and my sister—while I shuffle about to make a morning brew. I return to my nest, wrapped up in my duvet, tea in hand. By the time I'm comfortably settled for another day on the coach, the next headline is underway, full of flashing ambulance lights and the livid red of a fire engine. I turn the sound back on.

'...in the care home were safely rescued by emergency

services, save for one man. Ninety-three-year-old Arthur Shipton was pronounced dead at the scene after firefighters had to force entry to his room on the third floor...'

Coincidences always freak me the fuck out, and this one's a killer. Only yesterday, I was cramming myself full of chocolate biscuits and thinking about Arthur, and today he's as dead as dust. I wonder if the fire started when I was thinking about the home? Like I have some sort of pyromantic memory that whenever I think of the past something goes up in flame. I should check on my ex-mother-in-law—see if she's dropped her cig in her lap yet.

So, this is what happened: sometime between midnight and 2 a.m., a fire started on the second floor of the east wing in a disused room filled with those shitty old wooden chairs we were made to suffer at primary school. Ample fuel for a fire. It travelled upward and found its way to the third floor, mostly the M. Hopkins Corridor. Smoke gusted out the windows like a belching dragon, and the orange glow of the fire from its belly rebelled in heavy gusts against the firefighters' sprinkle of piss. The night staff were quick to wheel out the inmates and load them into multiple ambulances and vans. Room 9, though, where Arthur was sleeping soundly, deaf now and near fully blind, was engulfed in flame. When the alarm had first been raised, a nurse on his corridor had tried to open the door but the key had somehow snapped off in the lock; the security guard, one of those bald-headed, beer-belly guys who never expect to see any action, gave it a go next and broke off the handle by accident, so he launched his shoulder against the door, banged his head on the frame, and knocked himself out. That left the firefighters, when they arrived, to break down the door and carry Arthur's body to the useless safety of a stretcher.

Watching the story unfold with the brew between my hands and sitting cross-legged on the couch, a woman about my age appears on screen. Stella Shipton—Arthur's granddaughter, apparently. A patch of hair above her right ear is shaved, while the rest is long and waved and deep brown, swept to the side, blustering in the breeze. Her exposed ear is dotted with studs, and a silver star hangs from her earlobe. Not one glimmer of surprise or sadness seems to have stolen upon her face. She replies to the reporter's questions politely enough, though to me she looks bored. She lives with her two aunties on his old farm, for which she will be eternally grateful. She has happy memories of his cows, three of which he kept even after the farm shut up shop. His cremation will be held in a week.

I pause the TV on her image. Most of the time when you pause people mid-chatter on TV their mouths hang loose as if the wires have come undone, and with it comes the unveiling of additional chins. Just like the photos my mum likes to take, the *au natural* shots when my sister and I are about to bite into a chicken wing, or when we've fallen asleep on the couch. Stella, though, she's a butterfly pinned in a photo frame. Strands of hair have blown across her face, frozen now like thin twigs on trees caught by frost. There's a tattoo on her neck, just below her earlobe, of a simple triangle. I wonder why.

I wonder, too, what Arthur thought of her. He, the traditional dairy farmer in his woollens and flat cap and thick Yorkshire accent, and she, pierced, semi-shaven, flatly spoken; a different kind of woman.

He didn't approve of tattoos, I remember that much. Sarah had loads of them, and as soon as he spotted her sleeve—nothing to be impressed by, since they were done by a drunk mate who liked stick men—he told her he would like to cut her arm clean off. She laughed it away, but later that afternoon when I collected his dinner plate and cutlery, I had to hunt about his room for the gravied knife. "I don't have nothing I didn't come here with, lass," he said, pursing his lips at me.

I never did find that knife. What I did find instead, under the bed in an old wooden box with velvet lining, was an ornamental pistol. How he'd smuggled that to the home, fuck knows. When he saw me handling it, he put a long, gnarled finger to his lips. "That's for the damned ravens," he said. I thought better of taking it away, so I snapped the lid shut and slid it back under his bed. Of course, he knew it was me who reported him to Matron Gray. It took a lot of custard creams to get him to calm down after she'd barged her way into his room with high-pitched squawks of chastisement.

I flick off the TV but the rest of the day my thoughts hover about Stella and Arthur and, inevitably, loom grudgingly back over to David, too. He has made a den in my head and hisses at me like a strangled snake. He got punched once, at the end of a night out in Halifax, by the doner kebab man; he chipped a tooth and was left with a little whistle whenever he said an *s* sound. At the time I had been hysterical, as any drunk woman would be when her then fiancé was randomly punched in the face by the doner kebab man. I still don't know why he'd been assaulted, but I doubt I'd give two fucks now.

But he's in my head today and I can't shake him. He keeps track of the days we have been unofficially divorced: four-hundred and sixteen. He reminds me it's been nearly a month since I left my job as a teaching assistant at the local secondary school. Never mind that I was a fully qualified lab tech. I got the job after I moved back home to Bradford, closer to mum—further from him. Odd choice, for someone who's timid and doesn't like kids. I can say anything I want about why I came here, but David's kettle-whistle hiss says it's because I fucked up the bills and couldn't hack it in a house of my own. Because I need him, but he never needed me. *Who would?*

I imagine him, as I always do now, in his lab coat, huddled in his university office and hunched over a graph, while his young girlfriend sits naked on the corner of his desk. He looks up from his paperwork, grinning in that way he used to do when he had too much beer, all wet and limp. Eager but ineffectual.

Who would even want you?

I can never answer back, no matter how hard I try.

I spend my day, mostly, like the many days before. A blur of my own four walls, thoughts full of nonsense dulled into silence by too much chocolate. It's not really a food coma I'm after—more like a lobotomy by sugar.

The most eventful part of the day is a bath. I don't even have any bubbles. I've drunk the rest of the cider already and I really want the smell of pickled onion crisps off my fingers. I fill the bath to the brim to ensure I'm properly submerged and then I do what children do and see how long I can hold my breath under water until it hurts my heart and my lungs thrash. It's the only thing left that makes me feel alive.

3

I curl up on the couch, under my blanket. Shuffling through my phone, I open up Facebook, a glutton for punishment. I want to look, I want to see them, see that they're sad and she got fat but not as fat as he's got—which is to say, that they're both fleshier than me, even after several mounds of parkin and packets of crisps and nightly bottles of booze over the last year or so—but of course they'll be as magazine-glossy as ever, the Instagram couple of the year. Never mind the age gap. The wage-gap. The lecturer-student gap. David is basically Leonardo DiCaprio, if he were a sports-scientist in Leeds.

Scrolling down the page, a new advert pops up: Goblin Market. It's different to the other ads I get, which used to be all about babies after I got married, and then they jumped right into dating ads after my relationship status changed. Lately they've presumed I've declared permanent spinsterhood, and have taken to advertising massive jumpers with cats on them and grow-your-own-vegetables. But Goblin Market sticks out. The picture is a black and white illustration of two long-haired women embracing, one resting her head upon the shoulder of the other as they sleep under the watch of strange little creatures. I click onto the page, and the information is scant, reading only, *Come buy, come buy. Curiosity shop in Haworth, run by the Shipton Three.*

Weird. I must've been reading about the news, about Arthur and the care home, on my phone or something, only I don't remember having done so. I swear sometimes Google just reads my mind. The algorithms are uncanny like that. *The Shipton Three.* Stella, I guess. She said in her interview about living with her aunts. Perhaps it's the three of them, two older women and their boho niece, running an obscure little shop to pay for the essentials. I imagine them on Arthur's farm, all dressed in dead-black, eating fresh eggs around the kitchen table as they chatter about him. I don't imagine they reminisce fondly. I imagine Arthur is, to them, as David is to me: an unwelcome creature with teeth and nails digging into their skin.

There's nothing else on the page at all, just the name, the picture, the description. And the location.

I get out of my old clothes and get dressed. Nothing too extravagant, of course. Just jeans and a hoodie and a spray of air freshener (I've run out of perfume). I even brush my teeth and put deodorant on. This feels better, this movement, this assemblage of a human I've put my face to.

In the car, I type in the postcode for a car park in Haworth and follow the satnav. My grandma used to drive us there when we were kids, but when my sister was old enough to stay at home alone, she always preferred to leave us to it. She didn't like the quiet drive along the winding roads through the old little villages like I did. While my grandma and I sucked on lemon bonbons, our favourite sweet, I would watch wayward raindrops trickle down the windows, sitting on my hands as I waited for the clusters of cottages to disappear behind us and for the moors to emerge through the mist. We made a game of counting the trees, lonely and secret beneath the veil of the grey sky.

It's not so bleak today, but it feels bleak. Or perhaps that's just my mood. I've never driven there myself, so I focus on the satnav's demands, leaving the trees unaccounted for. It's not the same without the lemony dust of sugar between my fingers, the long wait for the toffee centre to soften enough to chew. It's not the same journey without my grandma.

Haworth is built on a steep hill where the wind is fiercest—windy enough to blow out my grandma's lighter over and over, until she threw it to the ground one time in a tantrum and popped another lemon bonbon in her mouth, and from then on never bothered to smoke when we got there. We liked it best in the late autumn, when the colours had turned from green to red to brown, when the cold called for hats and scarves and hot chocolate in a flask. There were fewer tourists at that time, so it felt like it was our secret place.

David has never been, never went with me when I asked him to. He's a city man, cut from the hard edges of square modern buildings, not a hint of history in him but the vague idea of a golden age of the *before*. I'm something in-between: born in the bleak vibrancy of twentieth-century northern England, I grew up feeling out of place, out of time, never quite in my own skin, drawn to another light I can't even see, like a blind moth.

When I park, I suddenly feel stupid. This human I've assembled doesn't want my face. I start to pick myself apart, sitting in the driver's seat, clutching the parking ticket I've just bought from the Brontë Parsonage Museum car park. I forgot to brush my hair: I forgot to *wash* my hair in the bath last night. I haven't put a scrap of makeup on. Haworth might be used to the eccentrics—the quaint Yorkshire folk who always look like they've just wandered off the moors even if they've never stepped foot there; the retro-rockabillies, glamorous and suave; the swarms of swanning elderly folk—but Haworth is not used to me. *I* am not used to me.

I can't breathe. I sip and sip and sip the air like water, and I drown in it. I put my head between my knees, jammed up against the steering-wheel. I'm screaming in that soundless way people do when they're underwater: there's nobody to hear, and the bubbles of my breath burst before they reach the surface. David's hands are on me, pushing me down, a dead weight. His hands are everywhere on my skin, trying to re-mould me, make me liquid so he can pour me into a new shape, because I am not enough; I am too much flesh. I pinch my arms and thighs, dig my nails into myself. The pain makes me more solid. This pain is mine; I inflict it; I carve myself alive.

Finally, I breathe normally. I won't go back home and hide. I am here to check out Goblin Market. Maybe see Stella. Not that I have a clue why I want to see her, or what I want to say. I just have this desire to be near her. I haven't felt this kind of hunger in years. Cake and cheap wine won't satisfy it, that's for sure.

Outside, the air has that special kind of fresh scent that you get out in the countryside. It's warm and reviving, with only a whiff of a fart. There are flocks of white-haired Yorkshire folk, heading for The Wool Mill Shop at the top of the hill. My grandma and I used to visit the teashop, where she'd test a different cake each time, thumbing every crumb from her plate. Her parkin was always the best though: that was not allowed to be tried and tested.

I make my way to the high street through the narrow, cobbled path between the museum and the old school rooms, hands in my pockets and head down. The school room is empty and dark from within unless you press your face close to the arched windows to peer inside. I once went to the museum one summer with school. I mostly remember how cold it was despite the warmth outside, and shuffling in my skirts to cover more of my legs, partly to keep warm but partly to hide my hair before the sunlight could catch them—before my classmates, suddenly much older and wiser than me, would see that my mother wouldn't let me shave yet. She'd told me the night before that Charlotte Brontë wouldn't have shaved her legs.

I spent the rest of the visit reading *Wuthering Heights* outside, sitting on the cemetery wall. How romantic, I thought, to be loved so intensely by a man like Heathcliff. Clearly, I was too young to understand. I can't say I'm too young to understand love, or men, or even myself, anymore. I don't think I understand much at all, and I've almost forgotten why I've come to Haworth in the first place, until a squawk breaks through my reverie.

Wind wends its way along the little street, disturbing the

rooks in the trees of the cemetery. It's one of those old graveyards where you can hardly read a word on the moss-covered stones, and the ground is bulbous, swelling with centuries of bodies and the tangle of roots. A bird swoops down from its perch with an indignant flourish of its wings, landing on the wall, its little eye fixed on me as it hops along. It cocks its head contemplatively, as if to view me from a different angle to get a better measure.

"You've got yourself a shadow," a man says, startling me. For a moment I think it's Arthur, tall and stately, flat cap askew on his head. But then the old man smiles, flashing a missing front tooth. Arthur's teeth were neat and white. Besides, Arthur is dead.

I smile thinly at the stranger as he steers his wife into the pub at the top of the main street. When I look over my shoulder, the rook nods at me, as if satisfied, and takes off with a squawk.

I head down the steep cobbled lane, passing dog walkers and ramblers on their way to lunch at the cafes, peering at the shop signs as I meander. The old sweet shop, a place that looks like an apothecary, and the retro shop coloured in the purple and green of suffragettes. There's an old red telephone box, a relic from some other time. There's the silver shop, the chocolatier, half-a-dozen antique shops. I get right to the bottom without seeing Goblin Market.

I look up the hill, confused. It can't be anywhere else. I must have missed it. All the little buildings look similar from this vantage; the guttering and frames are all painted black, the stone bricks darkened by pollution. I can hardly read the jutting signs swinging in the breeze.

With a sigh I brace myself for the thigh-burning hike back up the hill, taking my time to stop outside each shop door. There are fewer people outside now, and the top of the hill is furrowed with low hanging clouds. We never do get much of a summer up in Yorkshire. I stuff my hands in the pockets of my hoodie, keeping my head bowed low as the wind licks down the high street. Left and right, there's no sign of Goblin Market.

The bloody heavens open. Did I even check the forecast? Probably not. It's pissing it down, soaking my hair and my jacket, making it cling uncomfortably to my arms. The universe's way of telling me to get a proper shower. I linger in the rain as everyone else makes a mad dash for the nearest café or shop door, wondering if I should just keep marching on, get home, and get under the blanket again. But then I realise someone is shouting at me.

"Oi, love, come inside!"

I look to my left. A woman, all in black, is waving at me from the doorway of a shop. Goblin Market. I don't know how I could have missed it: the name is bold and black above the crimson door, and the sign that swings back and forth has those strange creatures I saw in the illustration on the Facebook page. On this scale, I can see more clearly that they're marching down a hill under a starry sky, carrying baskets of fruit. Their peculiar bodies are almost human in shape, but their faces are animalistic with long snouts. There's something almost cartoonish about them, but that just makes them more grotesque.

I dart inside the shop, the jingle of wind chimes announcing my arrival. Funny how the shock of rain can take your breath away. There's so much water dripping from my fringe that I can hardly see. The room is dark, and small, and crammed full of random objects from floor to ceiling. Pendants on string, crystals, pewter ornaments—a set of false teeth wearing a pair of broken glasses sits on a table, along with what I sincerely hope is not a real hand with candle wicks at the fingertips. There's a strong whiff of incense, and a heavy, musty scent that I can't identify. It reminds me of the old Gothic shops I used to steal cheap rings from as a teen, those kind of rings that make your fingers green at the end of the day.

"You must be soaked to the bone," the woman says. She passes me a cloth to dry my face and hands.

"Thank you," I reply. Now that the weight of rain is no longer in my eyelashes, I can see her properly. Her thick black hair reaches her waist, her eyes are big and brown, and her smile is warm. A dainty stud glistens on her right nostril, and her arms are adorned with countless bangles. "Are you one of the Shipton Three?"

"Goodness, no—I'm Nadiya. They're busy arranging their father's funeral. Seems to me all this rain is trying to put out that fire in the care home. Did you hear about it?"

She seems the kind of woman who relishes a story, so I let her ramble at me about the fire, secretly and strangely disappointed I didn't get to meet Stella. She chatters at me amiably, telling me about how she woke up to a hasty call, asking her to mind the shop, which was fine so long as she found someone to look after the boys, which she did, because the neighbour was happy to if she got some curry in exchange, so now when she gets home she has to make an extra portion of curry for the neighbour, though she worries it will be too hot since she's been round for dinner before, this neighbour, and couldn't even cope with what she'd called *pompadoms,* which the boys thought was hilarious, whereas she thought it at least mildly racist, but what can you do about old Yorkshire widows? Eventually Nadiya winds her way back to Arthur and the Shipton family, and it's then that I really tune in.

"I didn't even know their dad was still around. Never heard a word about him, or their mum. Stella is always the quietest about family life, but she's a nice girl. She came to check I was okay earlier this morning, and hardly seemed bothered her grandfather had died. Almost the opposite. Like nothing had happened at all. Said she was just eager to get on with everything. But, y'know, the strangest thing happened while she was here."

She leans closer to me. "We were chatting away, and she seemed pretty chilled out. Told me there'd be a service, but the after-party, or whatever you call it, was for family only, up at t'farm. And then she stopped talking all of a sudden, and her face went pasty white. I says to her, 'You look like you've seen a ghost.' She doesn't even reply. She just marches straight for the counter, picks up a flat cap, and storms back out. I don't have a clue where that hat even came from."

I smile, agreeing that it was strange, but couldn't help but think it was simply a coincidence, and not really the kind to freak me out. I'd already seen a man in a flat cap that morning. Sure, it's not so popular anymore, even in Yorkshire, but there's been some renewed interest, thanks to *Peaky Blinders*. Could have just been left behind by a customer.

The rain has stopped, and so has Nadiya's chattering. She stares at me now, with her big bright eyes and smile. "Well?" she says.

I blink. "Erm?"

She gestures with a sweep of her arm around the shop. "Going to buy anything?"

4

I shower properly when I get home and manage to cook for a change. Nothing fancy, of course, just pasta. I settle under the blanket on the couch, aimlessly scrolling through Netflix for something to binge, when my phone beeps with a text message. This time, it's actually David.

I got promoted to Reader! Drinks on Friday at Hop Scotch, 8pm.

And just like that, my sense of achievement for the day evaporates. What, after all, had I even managed to accomplish? I went to Haworth and came back with a tacky necklace, had a shower, and cooked for a total of ten minutes. Better get the biscuits out again. *He* got what he wanted. Again. What do I get? Sod all.

Friday night. I'll have to tag along, peck his cheek, smile. The charade that we are still married ended some time ago, but he's still keeping his girlfriend a secret from senior management, and pretends that our separation is amicable. The last thing I want to do is go congratulate the bastard while a crowd of ex-colleagues ask how I'm doing, feign interest in my spinsterhood, whisper about my weight. I could lie through my teeth: my new boyfriend is a pilot, which means I get the peace and quiet I want half the time, and glorious sex when he's around. He's a generous lover, you see, knows not only how to push my buttons, but he can find them in the first place.

I snort. I wouldn't be able to convince a dormouse.

Maybe I cry. A little. The promotion is my last tie to David, technically. The divorce can go ahead now—nothing to stop it. I shouldn't have let him delay it, of course, but I never could say no. Not really because of any puppy-dog-eyes influence, just my unwillingness to disappoint. Chronic people-pleaser, easy to sweep up with the dust. My first date after separating from David was with a comic-book nerd who totally ignored my quiet confession that I did not have a preference for DC or Marvel, since I disliked both equally; he proceeded to hero-worship the Hulk for at least twenty minutes before thrusting his mouth upon mine. I can't be certain, but I think green was his major turn on. Whatever had prompted the assault of his lips, I sat and tolerated it. I tolerated him pawing at my body.

All that happened right here, on my couch. I can't bear it. I decide to take a drive before more memories surface. I have no real destination in mind, no need for any more random sugar from the co-op. I just drive in the dark trying not to think of bad dates, or David.

Naturally that's impossible. My head is his second home; he's got an armchair in the corner. I'm stuck remembering that time when we argued over who had it worse as a kid. I wasn't arguing, really, just dumbfounded that he was so angry about the mere suggestion that I, or anyone else, might have felt the sting of an absent father like he did.

My dad passed away when I was a toddler, so I don't remember him much at all; just got this photo of him with a big beard and smiley eyes. Mum doesn't often talk about him, but I know he was a plasterer by day, taxi driver by night, and his favourite drink was a tot of brandy. My sister says he wasn't home much but reckons that was because he had to work so hard for us, since mum was so sick during both pregnancies and then got terrible depression after my birth. She got much worse after he died from some bizarre work-related accident I never really did understand. A few months after his passing, grandma stepped in, all no-nonsense and stiff upper lip with her sleeves perpetually rolled up to the elbows—a walking poster for the quintessential British *keep calm and carry on* in a matching M&S blouse and skirt—and taught me how to bake while my sister went to school and mum went to train to be a nurse.

But David's dad was one of those typical absent dads: around for all of the two required minutes, and gone for the rest. His mum wasn't even married to him, which was still worth a minor scandal back then, especially to her weirdly religious family who threatened to contact the police if he came near her again and promptly set her up in a dingy little back-to-back and then had nothing to do with her after. Some man he called Uncle Graham, a bank manager in town, took pity on her and gave her a job, and always sent flowers on her birthday. I didn't think it a good idea to tell David that his darling mother was obviously carrying on with "Uncle Graham", whose wife was headmistress at the local school and had that kind of mouth which looked like she could spit pins.

According to David, since my dad's dead, and I didn't know him, I've got nothing much to be upset about. He, on the other hand, had it so much worse. He's a guy; boys need a male role model, otherwise who's there to teach them how to play football and how to use a condom?

His rant was utter nonsense, escalating from virtually nothing. All I'd dared say was that I wondered if my nephew, newly born at the time, looked anything like my dad had as a kid. David threw a tantrum, so perhaps he's right: perhaps he would have learnt not to kick a television when he's pissed off if he'd had a father around. His apology, the next afternoon, came with the excuse that he didn't like hospitals and he thought we should have just waited for my sister to come home with the baby rather than visit. My fault, really. I even apologised.

The air is thin again, and I can only sip it, like I did before. It's in an acorn cup, and my lungs are tight, crushed. Before the panic washes over me entirely, I park at the side of a road. There's only one other car, a Ford, parked further up. When I realise I'm opposite the nursing home, the panic evaporates. I don't even know how I got here. I can't even blame it on autopilot; I've never driven here before. I always got the bus to work. I can only guess I followed the old route.

Hazard tape spans across the gates. Bouquets of flowers in plastic wrap line up against the wall, looking more like wet tissue and empty crisp packets in the dark.

I get out of the car to take a closer look. At night, without a single resident, the old building suddenly looks like some abandoned asylum or hospital. I peer through the iron railings, but it's so dark all I can make out is the silhouette. There's glass underfoot, crunching as I shuffle my feet. I wonder if I can smell smoke in the air or if it's just my mind playing tricks on me.

The gate rattles when I try to push it open, curious. Curious about what, I don't know. And I don't know where this interest has even come from. Leaving the flat, twice in one day? Unprecedented.

But the gate won't open, which is just as well; I'm sure it would count as trespassing if I did go in.

I thumb through the flowers, reading the labels instead. Generic sympathies, blessings, R.I.P. dedications. From Mabel, Keith, Mr & Mrs Hodgson, Nurse Buckley. I'm halfway through when I realise what I'm hoping to find: Stella's name. Some token from her, maybe. Nothing too special—she'd want to keep that for the cremation, maybe. I start to almost claw through the pile, tossing aside yellow carnations and limp tulips and pungent lilies. There's that feeling again, the panic that strangles the air—but it feels hotter this time, burning through me. It's not panic, it's desperation.

Under the pile of flowers, right at the bottom, I find a little black box. There's no tag or sympathies attached. It looks entirely out of place, like something forgotten at the bottom of a pocket.

There's a box of matches inside.

5

"I want to go to the cremation tomorrow," I tell my sister the next evening. Today's trip to the local shop has been more successful. Bag of chocolate, bottle of wine, pizza.

"Why the fuck would you do that?"

I regret ringing her. "You know. Respects, and all that."

"You worked there while you were at college, Kat. You didn't keep in touch with anyone. Morbid, is what you are. Is it some weird way of getting David's attention? Look, I know you're not happy right now, but pretending you're on top is far better than showing you're at rock bottom, love. You gotta fake it till you make it, y'know?"

Her advice is always just like this—parroted sayings. She's got that older sister's habit of lecturing me, which is fine; I tune out most of the time. Mum says she means well, and I suppose that's why I've rung her. I just want to listen to her. In some way, telling someone I've got plans makes me commit to them, even if I'm told it's a stupid idea. Soon after advising me to move on, with the added helpful reminder that it's been over a year, and perhaps a nice walk in the fresh air would solve everything, she commences her usual chat: the DIY she's instructed her husband to complete, her arguments with the southern HR woman, the terrible choice of local nurseries for her son. They're all actually pretty decent, but her little monster is a precious angel who does not, in fact, bite other toddlers. He does bite adults, though.

A month or so before it all finally ended, we were playing happy families, only mum knew something was off in that preternatural way mums do, so she did her usual pantomime theatrics at dinner as if everything was super-duper fine, which put everyone on edge. I sat quietly drinking wine and eating ice cream with my nephew on the floor of the dining room, sorely tempted to pinch his chubby little arm so that he'd cry and put an end to the tension before someone else cracked. I didn't, of course. What happened instead was his first bite.

David had decided it was time to go home—his clock-watching had never been subtle, and I was often in trouble for imposing the torture of a minute with my family upon him—but my nephew disagreed. When David bent down to take my arm, the little demon bared his fangs and sunk his teeth into David's forearm. He shook him off like a dog.

"You little shit!"

David was quick to retract his insult in the face of my sister's fury. He never did back down from an argument with me, though. He could wield his mind like an axe, cutting down parts of me he didn't like with a scientific rage he had twisted to his own tastes. I always drove him to it, though; that was the catch. I often found myself apologising for something I didn't understand, which was part of his trick—to make me feel stupid, like he did know what was better for me, and that's really all he wanted. It's like he hollowed me out of all my stuffing and put his hand in my throat, like a sock-puppet, so I could apologise for my *selfness*. He couldn't do that to my sister, though. She outmatches him. He's a lecturer, she's a CEO. She has the higher paygrade.

So he had no choice but to hang his head and apologise. The drive home was a particularly silent one. I don't even remember crying at that point, though. We got home, I went to bed. He trashed the house, tore the wardrobe down, punched in the light-switches. Ripped up my journal. The next morning, the elderly neighbour came over and asked to see me. I stood on the doorstep for inspection as she checked for bruises on my face. She promised to ring the police the next time she heard such a riot. David left for the rest of the weekend after that, leaving me with my humiliation, just got in the car and drove off. He came back late Sunday night smelling of perfume.

I don't want to think about that. I try to focus on my sister, and the muted show I've put on the TV—I need noise and words like I need air, to shut out my own echoes sometimes. It doesn't work. The clang of cutlery hits my ears as David targets the kitchen. I take a sip of wine and try to think of something else. Goblin Market. Stella. Her grandfather, Arthur.

It was his temper that made the others nickname him the Devil. The only nickname I've given David is a Sean Bean *bastard*. When I knew Arthur, his voice had been strong and clear, sonorous, like I imagine a Victorian headmaster would have sounded before he wracked knuckles with a ruler. Or unleashed the whip. He could make his voice ring along the corridor, rousing the inmates in an almighty cacophony. Whenever he had a lucid moment, when he would blink his crinkling eyes and realise he was in a nursing home, he would jump to his feet and stride down the corridor, banging his fist on each door repeatedly, shouting, "Out! I want to get out!" A chorus would rise up: "Out, out, out!"

He wasn't always on the third floor with the other Andy Dufresnes. He got out, my first day of work. I walked in the door, and he strode right past me. Straight-backed, smartly dressed, towering. He had a cane with him, but it seemed only an accessory to that Victorian headmaster's look, not a walking aid. Definitely had his flat cap on. I didn't give him a second thought as he marched across the road. Busy checking-in for my first shift at reception, two men in scrubs came hurtling down the corridor, shouting his name. The chaos that ensued could rival a soap opera, or a farce. I still don't know if this is a drama or a comedy.

Other biscuit bitches crowded about the window, thrilled by the distraction. The Matron barked at them to get back to work and to leave the lads to bring Arthur back again (this was his third, and final, attempt to make a break for it). Not that the Matron herself returned to work, either. They all watched, and I stood on my tiptoes at the back.

Arthur was sure-footed and fast. He pelted up the road, and then disappeared from view behind the wall. We heard tyres screech, beeping horns. Arthur reappeared, coming back down the road. His pursuers lagged behind, young as they were. Then they were in a triangular stand-off, the staff making gestures of calm, Arthur brandishing his cane.

He cracked one of them over the head; the man crumpled to the ground in the middle of the road. The other saw his chance and latched onto his caning arm, holding him back. Trouble was, Arthur was much taller than both those men. The tussle went on for some time, even when the other picked himself up off the ground. There was talk in the reception of calling the police for back-up, but nobody moved from their viewing station. In the kerfuffle, Arthur's flat cap fell off. That was enough distraction for him: he stopped his attack immediately and scurried about to retrieve it, but the lads would have none of it. They swooped in and hauled him back inside—to the applause of the other inmates, who whooped and cheered as he past them, swearing like a sailor. Every word in the book, even the *c*-word.

I went about my shift making tea. The whole bloody day. I tried making friends with the other biscuit bitches, but I never have grasped how to make myself popular or to fit in. When I left at seven, huddling in my hoodie and eager to grab a chocolate bar from the shop by the bus stop, I saw Arthur's flat cap still in the road. I didn't think it fair to leave it there. I felt sorry for him—for all of them. Care homes smell like hospitals, and they have about as much funding as them, too. It was drab and musty and everyone spoke to them like children. It's kinda why I prefer to call them *inmates*: thinking of the elderly like they're young adults with electronic ankle tags gives them some agency in the mischief they get up to, that kind of reckless, wilful, energetic rebellion against their own state of being that thinks itself untouchable, immortal.

So I picked up the hat, shaking off any dirt and damp from the road, and go back inside to Arthur's room. I peered round his door and found him sitting at the window, dreaming of his earlier glimpse of freedom. I hadn't seen his records, so I didn't know if he was deaf, but he didn't hear me come in (I learnt later that his hearing was fine; he was just stubborn). I cleared my throat. "Arthur? Arthur—I have your hat, though it might be a bit damp."

He turned to look at me. His eyes were dark, impelling. The delighted smile was eerie. He held out a steady hand to take it from me. He put it on his head, patting it down to the shape of his skull. He didn't say thank you or anything. Just kept his eyes on me, with his thin, purplish lips stretched into a grin.

As I was about to leave, he said: "They've done this to me, you know. They've put me here."

"Who has?"

"My daughters. Witches, they are. The lot of them. This is the thanks I get for keeping a roof over their heads."

I tried to placate him before he got too mardy. I didn't see his cane in his room, luckily, though that gun of his was probably hidden somewhere, waiting. I'm glad I didn't know about it at the time. "I'm sure your daughters are doing what they think is best for you."

He scoffed. "They want my farm, I know it. They aren't going to inherit anything from me, I promise you that. None of them. I should've had a son. I shouldn't have been so soft on them. I won't let them come visit me, now they've put me here, in this hell. Witches, the lot of them." He continued to mutter to himself, patting his head, his flat cap—*the most Yorkshire of all personal talismans*, the woman at Goblin Market had laughed. The talisman she bade me buy is around my neck now, just a smooth amethyst pendant she said would guide me to self-realisation. Twenty quid for self-realisation isn't bad, I suppose. That's what I get for telling her about my non-divorce.

That's partly why I want to go to the service tomorrow—I want to know if he'll be cremated in his flat cap, though I guess cremations aren't exactly open casket. But it's not really just that. It's Stella—I want to meet her, or just see her. I came back from Howarth disappointed that I hadn't, or any of the Shipton Three. And then last night, outside the nursing home, and that box of matches among the flowers. The whole thing is weird.

I don't know where this curiosity about the family has come from, why her image has been so entrancing. I hardly have a clue what I'd say if I even met her. I just know that I've spent so much time feeling emptied out like a bucket with a hole at the bottom, trying to hold on to the sand as the tide comes in, that this unexpected spark of wonderment is better than treading water.

I don't tell my sister I went to Goblin Market or took a late night drive to the nursing home when she finally gets round to asking me how I am and if I have done anything lately. She asks me the question lazily, knowing I seldom venture out. I tell her I wandered up and down Haworth high street for a while in the afternoon, that I went into a café when it started pissing it down. I definitely don't tell her David got his promotion.

"I didn't even know it rained."

We have a petty row about the weather, and whether or not it rained just in Haworth or all over Yorkshire. We will probably do this when we're old, sitting in rocking chairs and staring out the window, the one of us always seeing rain, the other the sun. As we prattle on, I realise I can smell something. Something burning. "Fuck! The pizza. Love you, bye."

6

The next morning, I eat leftover burnt pizza for breakfast in the car on my way to the service. I'm late, but it doesn't matter much; I only want to creep in at the back. I try not to make an entrance, but of course the heavy door creaks. As I enter the whispering room my only response to the swivelling heads is to smile nice and big, and wave. I mouth *sorry* several times. All while grinning like a twat, at a funeral service. Arthur's coffin is up front and centre, shut, unsmiling.

I take a seat on the back row and sink down. I can just imagine my sister saying she told me so. Blood burns my cheeks, and no amount of wafting cools my embarrassment. Turns out I've used the order of service to cool myself off. It's like I'm fanning Arthur's flat cap at my face. To my right, on the opposite row, an older woman snorts. I can't tell if it's a snort of indignation, like older folk are so good at, or the suppression of sudden hilarity—but it's definitely aimed at me. The woman beside her, who seems that bit older with tufts of white hair peeking from the rim of a bloody ridiculous black-feathered hat, elbows her sharply in the side. There's a ruffle between the two of them, as they make a show of being quiet and dignified, facing forward again with straightened backs. I wonder if they're Stella's aunts.

People have been invited to say a few words which, in my experience, is never really just a few words. A woman almost leaps out of her chair and forces her way along the row, making a reluctant wave of mourners who jump to their feet, sucking in stomachs, to let her pass. When she reaches the end, she trips over someone's handbag, but this only propels her forward to the podium in even greater rush. She faces the crowd, flustered, adjusting her clothes. She clears her throat. "Um," she begins. She clears her throat again and ducks down, bringing her brightly lipsticked mouth to kiss the microphone. "I'm Nurse Buckley," she says, and the microphone screeches in protest. There's a ripple of discomfort across the room, of hands clasping ears. She adjusts herself again, settling back. She reminds me of a chicken.

She turns out to be the nurse who broke the key in Arthur's door. She has a lot to say about how sorry she is that it happened, and even more to say that it wasn't her fault. She tries to explain that she'll always remember Arthur fondly, but it isn't convincing. There's a lot of babble about how he could still walk around the corridors despite being blind and deaf. With a nervous titter, Nurse Buckley says that Arthur would often sneak upon the other nurses like a ghost, and they were all certain he knew damned well what he was doing, creeping along the corridor and scare them half to death. (Of course, she doesn't say his nickname). At the mention of ghosts and death she reverts to explaining that it really isn't her fault he got stuck in his room when it went up in flames.

And that's when Stella intervenes. She's tall, slender, and is wearing a long black dress with spaghetti straps. She almost glides to the podium, silent, but I think I spy a smirk playing on her lips. Nurse Buckley is quietly thanked and ushered back to her seat as sobs bounce upon her shoulders. Stella steps up to the podium, and I realise I am leaning forward in my seat. I force myself to relax, unsure why I am so intent on her. I can hear David's voice laughing in the back of my mind, scornful: *She's everything you're not.* I try to tell his voice he doesn't know me at all, but he always answers back: *You don't know yourself.*

His voice, though, is muzzled by Stella's voice. "Thank you, Nurse Buckley. That was... Thank you everyone for coming. The cremation will begin now."

I slump in my chair, strangely disappointed. Nobody else is invited to speak for Arthur. Flipping through the pages of the order of service, I realise that there really isn't much planned. Arthur's photo on the front looks stern, those purple lips of his pursed as if ready to scold. Of course, he's wearing his flat cap. But he's younger than when I knew him, maybe fifty, his face tanned by the sun and his eyes wide and dark, looking directly at the camera. It looks like a passport photo: severe, flat, soulless. On the next page, the music that opened the service—which I had missed—is listed as Johnny Cash, "The Beast in Me". That has got to be the weirdest song for a funeral. I imagine everyone piling inside, teary-eyed and hiccoughing, filling up the airy room to the lyrics, and in one sudden rush the despair of death rends their clothes, and they transform into slack-jawed, howling wolves. I am sorry to have been late. I would've liked to have seen the reactions of the audience.

Stella doesn't say anything else. The order of service only mentions the welcome by the officiant, a Ms Priya Mehta, and the invitation for non-family members to speak in honour of the dead after. An italicised note is underneath, explaining that the family decline to share their private thoughts at the public service, and will be hosting a wake at the farm, by invitation only. So that's it— I came to hear Nurse Buckley babble about old doors in the old nursing home. And to see Stella shoo her way.

The curtain behind Arthur's granddaughter slowly closes around the coffin. The whir of electric hums across the room, like a buzzing fly worn out from beating against a window for escape. Stella turns, ever so slightly, to watch as the coffin slips from sight. She remains at the podium until the thin slice of light from the closing curtain winks out. The silence is unsettling, and I get goose bumps on my arms, all the blood and heat from my earlier embarrassment sucked dry.

Arthur, behind the curtain, unseen, still seems to me to be ready to rip aside the veil and shout, *Out, out, out!* The air is choked, dry, waiting for someone to move. I feel almost itchy in my seat. Luckily, it's not Arthur's corpse who makes the first move. Stella strides down the aisle, her eyes locked on the door. Heads turn to follow her, and the older women, the ones who'd watched me, sigh heavily as she passes them by, shaking their heads. Of course, with their heads turned to follow her out, their eyes are fixated on the back of the room by the door—near me. In the moment Stella strides by, the two of us are both caught in their curious stares. Although I sorely want to study her, see her face up close, the colour of her eyes, I stare at my feet and try to make myself a shadow, out of the reach of everyone's gaze.

The officiant, taken aback, returns to the podium. She is respectfully senior—old enough to show deference to the aged departed, but young enough not to count herself among the waiting. "Thank you all for coming to celebrate the life of Arthur Shipton," she says. I detect some reluctance to use the word *celebrate* for the abrupt service. "The family are hosting a wake at the farm, for relatives only. They encourage everyone else to donate to help rebuild the nursing home. You'll find a collection bucket at the exit."

Music stirs. No random Johnny Cash this time—Elvis Presley, "Return to Sender". Another off-beat choice, but nobody seems to notice the irony of the chorus line, so I try not to smirk. Mourners stand up, most looking dazed, and file out. I linger in my seat, looking up at the faces as they pass by, trying to fathom who's family and who's something other, like me. Nurse Buckley totters by in her stilettos; the man beside her puts his arm around her, as if in comfort, but it seems to me it's to keep her steady. She's crying, and so are some younger faces, faces that look like they would have preferred to be somewhere else, faces with pale lines of foundation-rivulets dug out by uncomfortable tears. I guess they're staff from the home. I wonder if any of them are biscuit bitches. A man in a wheelchair nods courteously at me as he passes by. Other snowy-haired elderly folk inch past, jabbering among themselves, expressing their dismay at the lack of cake. Some make alternative arrangements and declare they will head to Fat Annie's down Market Street. They ferret in their handbags to dig out loose change and drop it in the red bucket, saving their fivers for a slice of carrot cake and coffee. One woman, trotting along with a tri-walker despite appearing to be ready to run for it if she were given half the chance, pauses at the door and thrusts a hand into a jacket pocket; I think it is to find cash for the charity collection, but instead she plucks out a hip flask and puckers her toothless mouth to take a swig. She notices me watching, smacks her lips together, and winks.

It's almost the end of the track and most people have already left, though I can hear a bumble of voices in the car park. A handful of women remain and are now edging along the rows, bouncing bottoms from one seat to the next like they were playing ten in the bed. This includes the woman who snorted at me and her companion with the ridiculous hat. They congregate together in the middle of the aisle, seeming not to have noticed I'm still present, and for some reason I feel it would be better to stay quiet rather than open the creaking door and announce my exit as I had my entrance.

"I did tell her to behave," the ridiculously-hatted woman says, folding her arms. The many layers of her clothes are long and baggy, the cardigan fraying at the edges. I realise now her hat is not just a mound of black feathers; it's a taxidermy raven. The beak, like her nose, is long and sharp.

It overlooks the brim of her hat on the right side, as if on guard. Impressive, but still bloody weird.

The women collectively shake their heads in disapproval. One, a stout, Afro-haired woman in dungarees, replies, "Flippin' 'eck. She's a mardy mare. Should've saved her sulking for the wake."

"I wouldnae be surprised if this were all her doing," another woman says in a thick Scottish accent. She points a crooked, accusatory finger. "One of you two should've seen it coming."

"And what's that supposed to mean, Hazel?" the hatted woman snaps.

"Let's all calm down, sisters," says the woman beside her. I decide her snort had not been one of derision after all; her face, freckled and flushed, is too kindly for that. "Indeed, I think we are all still in a little shock. There's plenty of good food and drink back at the farm. The pyre is all set up."

They turn and make their way to the door and, for the first time, realise I am still sitting there. The two at the front stop first, looking at me with bewilderment. The women behind bump against them.

I stand up, feeling the weight of my body in the measurement of their eyes. I've done my best to look presentable—I even showered, the second day in a row—but I feel like a black helium balloon, an inappropriate and singular piece of decoration for a funeral. I can't speak while they're peering at me so intently.

"You're Stella's friend, aren't you, love?" the kind one says, extending her arm for me to take.

"Erm—yes, I'm Kat," I lie, with relief. I loop my arm

through hers. She isn't old or infirm, but the gesture is familiar, and puts me at ease.

She smiles warmly at me. "I'm Stella's Aunt Sybil. And this is my sister, Alma." The woman with the dead raven on her head nods curtly at me. "I wonder, if I could trouble you, to take the two of us back to the farm? We didn't think the old Rover would make it all this way and I fear Stella has taken the Ford already."

She takes me familiarly by the arm and escorts me outside. The other women fall silent and make their way to their own cars. Is this what I wanted to happen—to meet the Shiptons, to be welcomed in some way? Well, I know I wanted to meet Stella. I've spent so long simply drifting, treading water, drowning when the storms of memory wash over me, I don't know what it feels like to want. I don't know if I've swum toward the shore or let the tide pull me in, either—if I've let Stella draw me out or if I've sought her out. Both, I suppose.

I can't say no to such a friendly face anyway, so I find myself dusting crumbs from the car seats and scooping up rubbish from the floor before they clamber in. Alma sits in the front, her hat scratching the roof. I would've preferred for Sybil to sit beside me, but the seniority of her sister and her consequent right to sit shotgun seems not to be challenged. She does not say much to me but sits with her hands clutching the seatbelt as if I'm driving too fast, giving me last-minute directions to turn left and right. Sybil, on the other hand, is sitting squarely in the middle of the backseat, leaning forward to speak to me, without wearing a seatbelt at all.

"You mustn't think too badly of us. My father was a bit of a rascal, in his prime, and we are quite a private family," Sybil says. Her voice has only the slightest trace of a Yorkshire accent. She's quite prim. "And poor Stella, without her mother for so many years and a father who never did show up, and only us old dears knocking about in the farm for company. Indeed, I don't think she really knows how to process his death."

I am about to reply something sympathetic but generic when Alma crisply points ahead. "Down there."

To take the sharp left turn down the narrow road I break heavily. The car behind protests and overtakes with an angry gesture flung out the window. Neither Alma nor Sybil seem to notice. We journey some time as I follow the bends of the narrowing road, bullied into ditches by large four-by-fours that speed by while Sybil chatters about the history of the farm. Low-hanging branches of trees batter the left of my car, but as the road inclines further and I wind my way up through the moors, the hedges that line the road disappear and broken-down fences jut out from time to time, like the last few trembling teeth in a broken jaw. Hills bulge above on the left and burst below on the right of the road. The sun competes with the clouds to dominate the sky.

"Tell me, Kat—how long have you been divorced?"

I blink. "Erm, how did you know?"

She chuckles. "The bonds of marriage leave marks, as it were."

I look at my left hand. The finger is a little thinner, I think, where my wedding ring used to be, and paler, too.

Though I have spent plenty of nights in a bubble bath with a cheap bottle of wine, staring at the empty space, I never noticed it before. I take a deep breath before I answer. "Officially, not at all. But we separated last year, the day after my thirtieth birthday. He got himself a younger model. He's thirty-eight, and she's only twenty-two, fresh out of uni. David was her lecturer at Leeds—"

"Oh, no—no dear. The rules are: dead or divorced, men aren't discussed," Sybil interrupts me.

I smile. "I quite like that rule."

"Most women do. Now, at the wake, we will indeed be talking about Arthur, for a while. It's a family tradition of ours to have a big bonfire, get rip-roaring drunk, and tell tales. When the last embers die, we believe that is when the spirit is laid to rest, as it were." She crinkles her nose in a smile. "Something of a very old Yorkshire tradition."

"Oh," I say, as if I've heard of this native practice. It's not something my grandma ever mentioned.

"Right at the gate," Alma interjects.

I slow and turn down a battered road surrounded by a broken stone wall. I can see the farm emerge ahead, almost out of nowhere. I don't have a clue where I am. Cars are parked up on the gravel and grass. Women mill about, carrying chairs and tables from within the large old house out into the field.

Alma whips off her seatbelt before I've even stopped the car and is ready to lunge out. "Matilda!" she shouts as she opens the door upon the moment I pull on the handbrake. "You put that pot down! It's been in the family for generations, and I'll be damned if you smash it to hell!"

I linger, unsure whether I am supposed to join this private family function—if Sybil really has mistaken me for Stella's friend, if Alma will chase me away with a shaking fist in the air. But I want to stay and be part of this strange tradition. I still want to meet Stella.

"Come on, Kat," Sybil says, patting my shoulder.

"Erm, I don't actually know Stella," I quietly admit.

She's already out of the car and slamming the door against my words. I look about for my phone, tempted to ring my sister and ask what I should do—knowing what her answer would be anyway—when there's a knock on the window that gives me a start. Sybil is there, smiling and waving me to come out. "I know you don't know anybody—well, you know me now, and Alma, don't you?"

That settles it, I suppose.

7

Shipton Farm hasn't been a working farm since the eighties when it specialised in local delivery and historical demonstrations for school kids. It retained the proper old-fashioned way of milking—little wooden stool, a tinny bucket, and the tug of hands on udders—even back when it was first built in the mid-nineteenth century and industry made its move on farming. Not much money to be made out of such a means of milking, but the school kids enjoyed the demonstrations, especially after *Thatcher, Thatcher, Milk Snatcher* deprived them of the calcium. I never went as a kid, but I remember my cousin boasting about having made friends with a goat named Derek when he'd gone with his primary school one autumn. He'd not mentioned Arthur, of course. Sybil says it was her business in the nineties, before they'd shut up shop for good; I can just imagine her meeting kids with trays of ginger nut biscuits and happy chatter. I can't say the same of Alma, though. I imagine she kept watch somewhere, ready to intervene at the slightest hint of disorder.

Today the farm is the site of the weirdest family gathering I've ever seen. For starters, as far as I can tell, there's only women here, and most are older than me. I count about a dozen of them. A handful of rusting caravans are parked to the left, opposite the house, with the bonfire assembled between them. Their wheels have churned tracks in the mud, but most of the women are booted and sweep across the field without a thought for the roughened ground beneath them. There are two dogs off the lead, rushing between legs, yipping for attention. The choice of companion overwhelms them; the smallest, a wiry-haired mongrel, drops down in the grass to pant heavily. The springer spaniel continues to bound around in large circles, barking with glee. There's a mottled horse roaming, keeping out of the way, swishing his tail to rid himself of flies. I hear the honking of geese but can't see them. A wooded expanse crowns the field, climbing a hill, meeting the low-hanging clouds that threaten to drift toward the bonfire. The farmhouse itself, to the right of a crumbled stone wall overcome by weeds, looks as if it had once been neat, symmetrical, but now the brickwork is battered and turning black, and the little windows are crooked, sinking under the weight of the frowning roof. The wooden front door is red, but the paint is peeling, like lipstick on a cold, dry mouth. The small cowshed stands resolutely separate, with only holes where the windows and door had once been—abandoned and in disrepair, the perfect state of affairs for a horror film.

Sybil had told me in the car, that the farm had been in the family since the mid-1800s, but a fire had destroyed the old barns and half the house in the 1930s. Her great-grandfather had nearly died. His wife had been suspected of arson, but nothing much came of it, which was a good thing, since that would've put an end to the farm. I wonder now, taking in the view of the caravans and the bonfire and the house, with the women smiling and chattering as they bustle about, whether the female members of the family are pyromaniacs. I wonder if Stella is. If she left the matches among the flowers. I certainly didn't mysteriously set fire to the nursing home with my thoughts after one too many biscuits and an odd memory of Arthur and his hat.

Then there's the simple fact that the bonfire is not really a bonfire, or at least not like one that I've ever seen. For starters, it's raised up off the ground by big slabs of stone. I can't imagine who laid them all out, like some sort of altar. Atop is an unruly mass of broken wooden boards and slats, vaguely rectangular in shape, piled high. It's the size of the public bonfires hosted by the football club on Guy Fawkes night, and I marvel at the labour these women must have put into it. Larger posts stand at each corner, trying to cage in the chaos of the wood pile. Flowers are wrapped around them, tangled in thin rope; purple sage snakes along the broad beams, and great white lilies shout in random disarray. More flowers encircle the bonfire itself, with yellow winks peeking through thick weaves of blue wildflowers and broad sheaths of dill. I only recognise them from my sister's allotment, which I have been forbidden from touching ever again since I left her rhubarb patch to choke out everything else while she went on holiday last year. Allotments are only for those that have reached the not-so dizzying heights of Yorkshire success.

On the very top of the altar is, I think, a large door, laid flat. This is definitely not a bonfire; it's a funeral pyre, as if the cremation is due to take place right here, right now.

I stand back, watching the gaggle of women erect chairs and tables and load them up with piles of food and drink. These women, chattering like birds, flouncing across the farm as if it's mayday, only the pole is a funeral pyre for a man they didn't shed a tear for.

I don't know if I should help, or even what I'm doing there. I have a schoolgirl urge to find Sybil and ask her what I should do, and follow her brisk but gentle commands, but that would mean entering the fold. The woman in dungarees carries a large platter of cheese and quiche, closely followed by twins who have even dressed to match, each laden with pork pies, grapes, and a salad bowl. Alma has taken the role of overseer; she carries nothing but stalks a timid, middle-aged woman as she carries a tray of jam jars and clotted cream, directing her steps with crisp and sudden heckles, much as she had directed me in the car. Hazel, the Scottish woman, is close behind, and no sooner has the tray been laid where Alma has ordered it, does she move it, secretly, to a different location. Scones emerge later, along with an assortment of cakes, and boxes of wine. The smells are distant; the cool breeze wafts the scent of grass and mud, the scent of the earth that the cities have all forgotten.

The spaniel has found my legs. I crouch down to meet the bright face of the dog and receive the eager snuffle of his wet nose and the lick of his tongue against my cheek.

"Milton, take it easy!"

Ruffling Milton's floppy ears, I don't look up at the speaker. I know it's Stella, and suddenly I feel like I need this dog to hide half of me, make me smaller. I've left my jacket in the car; I have nothing to swamp me. Being conscious of the closeness of this willowy woman only makes me more conscious of my own body and the poor choice of clothes I have selected for a funeral, though this morning I had thought differently. I'd been almost proud to be washed and made-up and dressed smart. My dress is knee-length and blows about, threatening to flash that I'm wearing shorts underneath. Threatens to show I need them to keep my thighs from chafing. Not quite a little black dress, really. Worse, if it hadn't been for the dog rubbing his face in my neck and clambering up my torso, I would've forgotten that the empire line has settled uncomfortably beneath my bra. I'll be left with a red line in my flesh by the end of the day. I remember that the dress fit last year. There's nothing to distract from the fact that my cleavage is *right here.* The little crystal necklace around my neck now suddenly seems horrifically embarrassing; that morning I'd thought it apt, like a token of respect for the family, since I was invading the funeral, yet with Stella looking down at me I realise I look more like a stalker.

I want to pick up the dog, use him as a body shield. David, who's been quiet for most of the day so far, laughs at me.

Stella crouches down and strokes his head, making shush noises. I can smell her perfume. Orchid flowers. Between the two of us, Milton relaxes his excitement, and rolls onto his back between our feet for a belly rub.

"I'm Stella."

"I know," I say, before I could stop myself. I don't think

I'm breathing. "I'm Kat."

"How did you know my grandfather?"

"From the nursing home."

"Oh," she says, and pauses. I still haven't looked at her. "I didn't think we'd invited anyone from the home."

My cheeks flood. "Well, I somehow got roped into driving your aunts here and then Sybil sort of invited me. I don't reckon Alma knows I'm still here, though."

She laughs and stands up. Milton rolls onto his front and sits beside her. "Trust me. She'll know you're here. If she wanted you to go, she would've released the geese."

I stand up, smoothing my clothes and trying not to fold my arms over me as if I could hug myself further into myself. I wonder what she thinks of me. I wonder, too, why it seems so important. I can feel David's hands coil around my gut and twist like he's wringing out a wet towel. Trying to make me thin, thin like his student girlfriend, thin like Stella. Instead, he leaves stretchmarks across my stomach like the scars of his nails. I have a sudden urge to eat another packet of biscuits or bake a cake.

I can't avoid looking at her now that we are face-to-face. She looks at me, dark eyes wide and curious, with such intensity I cannot move. The breeze ruffles her hair; a few strands settle across her cheek and lip, so she tucks it behind her ear. The silence between us begins to feel awkward, and there's a look in her slightly arched brow that suggests she is waiting for me to speak.

"You know, we used to call Arthur the Devil at the nursing home," I say. Stupidly.

"So did we," she replies. There's a touch of amusement

in her voice, a ghost of a smile that makes me want to smile back. "But for very different reasons, I expect."

I hardly know how I find my voice, but I ask: "Will you tell me why?"

"If you get me drunk, I might." She has Alma's crisp, business-like tone of voice, but Sybil's soft smile. And there's something else, too. Maybe the shadow of Arthur is in her eyes, but they seem to burn with a different kind of energy than he had—his eyes had a ferocity in them which kept many of the biscuit bitches at bay, while her eyes have a glint of mischief in the making. If Arthur was the Devil, he was the kind that might smite with wrath; Stella was the kind that might smite with a smile. Funny, but I like that. I like her eyes.

She asks if I can help her carry a few things outside, so I follow her. There's casual confidence in the way she walks, and she gestures for me to keep up—to walk beside her. We reach the back door and enter the kitchen, which is large and rustic, with pots and pans hanging from hooks across old wooden beams. Every surface is covered with food. I can't help but notice there's no parkin, though there is a large Victoria sponge cake and a tray of flapjack bedazzled with raisins. The smells are glorious: meaty and sweet and tart, all at once. A homely smell. It was quite a feast for a dozen women. Stella sees the look of astonishment on my face and laughs, reassuring me that nothing will be going to waste.

Sybil enters the kitchen from another room, her cheeks bright and flustered. "Oh, girls—I didn't know you were in here! Why don't you take the boxes of wine, over there? All this is thirsty work, indeed!"

Stella takes a crate of wine, hardly noticing her aunt's evident nervous disquiet. Her smile is forced and fixed, and her head nods so rapidly I worry it will fall right off. Her hand is behind her back—hiding something. But I follow Stella out, carrying more wine outside, bottles chinking as we go. Sybil is close behind us, carrying nothing, but still has one hand behind her back.

"No, Stella! That's our summer wine—put it in the ice box, or you may as well pour it down the drain," Alma snaps.

"Well, where is it, then?" she replies.

"Over here, come on." Alma leads Stella away while I still trail a few paces behind them, less and less convinced I should be there. I can't help but think Alma is distracting Stella from something, though.

I glance over my shoulder. Sybil scurries to the pyre, looks about her to check nobody's watching, and thrusts something inside, deep into the heart. I swear it's a bloody flat cap.

8

The sunlight is fading, kissing the sky pink. Without the ceremonious bang of a drum or hoot of a trumpet, hush settles around me. The chatter stops, the eating and drinking cease, and even the dogs stop barking. They just all seem to fall into sync as the sun slinks low on the horizon, a sly, slow wink stretching across the farm. I've never known a quiet like it, so strangely loud with anticipation. Stella leaves my side, and the other younger women follow her into the old barn, while the senior women form a circle around the pyre like the points of a clock. I worry that I'm going to be the thirteenth—the unlucky, unwelcome addition. But Sybil, with only a whisper of her welcoming smile left imprinted on her face, takes me gently by the arm and stands me with her.

Stella soon strides out from the barn with sure and confident steps, carrying something white on her shoulder. Her young relatives walk in step with her, each sharing this peculiar white burden. I realise that they are bearing the weight of a cloth-wrapped effigy between them.

The blood in me swirls downward, pooling in my feet, and I nearly collapse, but Sybil holds me firm. It is not just the shape of a body; in the fading light, I swear I can see the silhouette of the strong jaw, the nose, the very features of Arthur sneering through the sheets that bind him tight. With Stella leading the way, they shuffle the body along the broken door at the top of the pyre, settling it in position, square in the middle, ready to burn. Stella strikes a match and drops it into a small bucket filled with briquettes and wood chippings, ready to light the torches.

Still, nobody speaks a word. They know their ritual by heart. A spectacled woman named Viv, the oldest of the gathered women, steps forward first, lighting her torch with a stony countenance, before she thrusts it deep into the prism of the pyre. Alma and Hazel, who have been battling all day to assert who's the senior of the two, both rush upon the pyre at the same time. The flames begin to eat away the wood, tentative, licking at the flavour of its meal. Next is Sybil, leaving me to stand alone, utterly dazed. Others take their turn in the same solemn, determined silence.

Stella seems agitated the whole time. Her gaze is fixed and firm upon the swelling gusts of fire while she shifts her weight from one hip to the other, impatient. She waits for the older grandchildren to feed their torches to the hungry mouth of the pyre, and waits still for Viv's and Hazel's own grandchildren. Stella, then, is last; the youngest present, in her early thirties, and the one most eager to burn Arthur's memory to ashes. Her torch is the last forkful of fire before the entirety of the pyre is swallowed whole.

I still cannot say whether or not I smell burning flesh. But I do know that I stand and watch and say nothing.

By midnight, I'm sitting in a semi-circle of strange

women who have huddled themselves in blankets, drinking wine and lager shandies from an assortment of mugs. The scruffy mongrel has settled with Viv, and Milton has fallen asleep at my feet, having grown bored of chewing my shoe. I've noticed a black and white cat saunter between the barn and the house a few times during the day, occasionally stopping to stare at the invasion of humans before turning stiffly away, tail indignant. There are lazy little flies drifting around the empty food plates, and moths are making their erratic descent toward the bonfire, curious about this earthly sun.

The fire is vibrant, almost vicious now. The orange glow shatters the dark sky, spitting embers. The dragon is back, I think to myself, irked that it didn't get one morsel from the nursing home, so it's come to finish Arthur off. Stupid thought, but I've had quite a bit to drink. So has Stella. She's stayed by my side for most of the afternoon, clutching my arm whenever a relative inched too close and opened their mouth to complain about her *little performance* at the service. She doesn't clutch my arm for protection though; she wields my strangeness, my out-of-the-family otherness, like a sword, and her eyes hiss, *I dare you*. I played along, smiling dumbly, though her hands around my arms felt hot enough to melt into me so that I wondered which one of us is going to sink into the other several times.

This grip of hers eventually loosened. Instead, she has taken to looping her arm through mine. Sitting now, side by side, with Milton at my feet and the heat of the bonfire shrouding my skin, it feel like Stella is planting me in the ground. I shake my head and take another sip of wine from my mug. I've had too many weird thoughts today.

"Stella tells me you called our father the Devil," Alma says, dropping down on the blanket beside us. Though she has removed some layers of clothing, revealing slender, speckled arms, she is still wearing her ridiculous hat. It reminds me of those cone party hats, and she seems to be just as proud as a kid, too.

I take a hasty gulp of wine, trying to bury my face in the mug.

Sybil rescues me. "Oh, Alma, don't tease the poor girl."

She snorts. "I'm actually relieved to know he got himself a reputation. Proves it wasn't just us who didn't like him."

Tentatively, I join the conversation. "He didn't seem to like you, either. Blamed you for putting him in the home and called you all witches." I recount my first day, when he'd tried to run off, and what he'd said to me about wishing he had sons. The words come pouring out before I stop to consider if it would upset them. But nobody—none of the Shiptons—had cried at the funeral service, only the people from the nursing home.

"You must think us cruel, leaving him there like that," Sybil says. There's sadness in her smile. "The truth is, even if he seemed hale and healthy, he wasn't. Ever since the accident, he got more and more paranoid."

"And vicious," Stella cut in. She doesn't look at anyone, only the fire.

Alma clears her throat, a silencer. She adjusts the raven on her head. In the firelight, the black feathers glisten, and the flicker of the flame-shadow makes it seem almost as if the bird is twitching, ruffling its feathers. Alma folds her arms. "We don't need to go through all of this. He was a vicious bastard when he was healthy, and a vicious bastard when he wasn't. Now he's dead. Leave it alone, Stella."

I'm torn. I can sense Stella and Alma are both resolute, sitting stubborn as statues, one inclined to talk as if storytelling will soothe memory of its sting, the other convinced silence will do the trick. But I want to hear Stella's side of the story.

"Why?" I ask. Stella still hasn't told me anything about her grandfather. Our conversations so far have been minimal, but the quiet hasn't been altogether uncomfortable. Whenever she asked me about my life, I was aware of the rule against the divorced and the deceased, and David's name never once slipped from my lips like purged spit. His voice in my head is subdued, perhaps pacified by all the wine, or maybe—and I prefer to think of it this way—shrunken in the face of so many women, as if the threat of menses and menopause could overwhelm him, blood being, in my experience, the only way he could define us. *The uncontrollable variable is not allowed in the lab.* He said that to me, once, when I tried to surprise him at work with lunch. Of course, I realise now, his sweaty brow and dishevelled lab coat had nothing to do with the flustered look of a Victor Frankenstein busy at work. He was just busy being sucked off by his student under the table.

"He was a traditional man, and a stickler for rules," Sybil begins.

Alma sniffs. "Only when it suited him." She gestures to the dozen women drinking around the bonfire. Hazel is still bossing Matilda as she gathers up discarded plates of unwanted salads and crumbs of over-baked bread. Viv has fallen asleep. I can't remember the names of the others at the moment. "He wasn't exactly faithful to our mother."

Stella picks at blades of grass by her feet. "He has six daughters. Rita's the youngest; she's only five or so years older than me. He was trying for a boy, you see, even in his fifties. Once a woman gave him a girl, he tried the next. When I was born, his only legitimate grandchild, he refused to talk to my mother. He's got four other granddaughters, but he was never interested in us, nor Syrah and Matilda, his great-grandchildren." She is staring intently at the bonfire. "The men of his family—"

"Don't go disturbing the dead, Stella," Alma snaps. Her hat is hanging low over her brow now; the raven shadows her expression and her words are carved in stone.

Stella throws the grass down at her feet. Milton licks them up. "The men in his family all lived at least to one-hundred. His father did, and his grandfather, and his grandfather's father."

"What about his wife, and all the other women and mothers?" I am unsure if I believe it all. Stella stiffens and, though we are barely touching, I can almost feel it, like I am suddenly sitting in the shadow of a tree and not a woman who can curve and coil and open. Her bare feet stretch and stir the earth, taking root.

"Our mother ran away with a soldier she once knew, when we were kids," Sybil says.

Alma snorts. "That's what *he* says."

The implication makes me wince. I glance at Stella,

trying to read her face. My eyes find the triangle tattoo on the nape of her neck. I wonder what it means, if Arthur is in the ink.

She looks at the circle of women surrounding the pyre. "My mother died when I was young. As for the rest of us, we will have to wait and see."

We fall quiet. The bonfire is loud, snapping bursts of ember as if the fire is disgusted by rotten wood and spits it back out. Earlier, the smoke of the sage bloomed into clouds, gently perfumed, but now the flowers have all been swallowed, almost whole, and the only crumbs left are charred deposits of ash coating the ground like black icing. The twins are singing, but the words are carried off, leaving only the melancholy notes of their song to whisper against the angry crackle of the bonfire. The voice of the woman beside them, a fifty-something bedecked in an elaborate scarf that twists around her scalp tightly, joins the chorus, but the notes clash. Hazel will not tolerate such a racket, and she tells them as much in sharp tones.

Someone else begins to sing—Matilda, the timid woman, evidently discovering in herself a rebellious spirit, as she sings loudly and with relish to mock Hazel's demands for quiet. With their voices, I can hear that they're singing Johnny Cash, the same song that played at Arthur's funeral, and as Stella joins in, I hum along with them. I am drunk, after all. They get louder and louder—disturb Viv from her slumber—and the dogs perk up; uncertain what to do, they howl. Stella jumps to her feet, shouting along with everyone, raging at the stars with melodic euphoria. I can't hum any more for laughing. Finally, Hazel gives up, and shouts louder and more tunelessly than the rest the final chorus line.

Laughter ripples like wind through a washing line, and I laugh so hard it hurts. I look at Stella; she is laughing, near hysteria. She throws her head back to share her sudden joy with the air.

Exhausted, I lean my head against her shoulder. Her skin is warm, the smell of the fire in her skin softened by her floral perfume. It isn't comfortable, as such—not like resting my head on a pillow, and my neck strains—but it is comforting. I yawn. I wonder how I am supposed to get home, knowing that I don't want to be anywhere but here.

9

I'm in her bedroom. Alma, to my surprise, has told me on no account should I attempt to drive through the moors in the middle of the night after having drunk so much unless I would like to kill myself, and if her niece were a half-decent human, which she was sure she could muster from time to time, seeing as though she had such excellent role models growing up, she would offer up her bed and take the couch downstairs. I said I would be comfortable on the couch, as I have been sleeping on my own for some time, but when Stella asked me what I would like, I changed my mind promptly and told her I would like to be in a proper bed but that we could share. I keep surprising myself today.

There are no lights in the room, but the curtains are pulled back, and the glow of the bonfire below sneaks through the window enough that I can make out Stella's silhouette as she discards her dress and pulls a vest over her shoulders. I am still in my own clothes with the smell of bonfire, sweet and smoky, resting in my skin and hair. Earlier, Sybil gave me an old t-shirt to wear to bed. The quiet acknowledgement that Stella's body was not my body made me wince. Now, watching her in the dark, seeing the straight lines of her back and arms and the small peak of her breast as she turns, I think reluctantly of David's student.

I imagine her tanned, all year, as if clouds and rain could not resist flushing her flesh with a glow the colour of a recent holiday—not the orange globular patchwork of self-tan I had tried to paste on my legs a few years ago, after David asked if I would make an effort (for *my* sake, of course) to go to the annual summer party at work. The painting of his young student fills me like sour milk: I see her legs, as hairless as her vulva, an invitation puckered there as she spreads herself open for him, and his hands, broad and flat, mould her belly and breasts like clay, shrinking her waist while pushing more flesh atop her chest until she is a Barbie of mud that titters when his beard brushes her neck. David is assembled in my mind like a dismembered body stacked up and waiting to be stitched together, all hard lines: first the feet, then the legs to the knee, the knee to his butt, then the back, the arms in shoulder sockets. His head crowns this jigsaw, a king of modern men.

"Are you okay?" Stella asks.

I nod and smile. I realise I've let a tear pierce through. To hide it, to pretend I'm fine, that I'm comfortable in my skin, I take off my dress in one swift movement and throw it down.

"What's wrong with your body?" Stella asks.

I freeze. "You serious?" She nods. I wonder what she means. The way she's looking at me, head cocked a little to the side, squinting in the dark, makes me think she's seen something I haven't yet discovered. This seems impossible:

I know every flaw. "Oh," I say, eventually, "You mean my scar? I tried climbing over the school fence when I was fourteen, but I got caught on the railing. I got seven stitches." I sound as if I'm proud of it, like it was some great feat of bravery to bunk out of P.E. with Mrs Senior, when really I just wanted to avoid Hayleigh who'd promised to hit me with a bat, just because. She's now a midwife. One of the reasons why I told David I didn't want kids. The truth is, I simply never imagined myself as a mum—it just isn't the sum of my ambitions. I don't remember what my ambitions are any more. There's only one right now, though: Stella.

She draws near me. "I didn't even see that." She is so close to me—so close I can smell the sweetness of her skin, feel the warmth of her breath upon my face. So close I wonder if she can hear my heartbeat, and desperately hope that she can't. Her fingers trace the jagged white line of my war wound around the curve of my waist, feather-light.

"Oh, good. That means you can't see my stretch marks," I reply. I want the floor to yawn open and swallow me whole. David laughs at me, in the back of my head. I always bring attention to the worst parts of myself. "They're not the good kind of stretch marks, either."

"The good kind?"

"You know. From pregnancy," I reply. She blinks, confused. Either she doesn't have any, or she's starting to realise I talk utter shit half the time. Maybe she'll just think I'm drunk. I rush to explain. "Not all stretch marks are from baby-baking. Some are just from plain old baking. And then eating. I've seen some women tattoo their stretchmarks in rainbow colours. The beauty of motherhood, and all that. The celebrities are at it, too. Even the Kardashian clan. Everyone was ranting and raving about the K-creature's 'brave' photo of post-baby stretchmarks on her boobs, but you'd need a magnifying glass to see them anyway." My mouth feels dry. I can tell she isn't understanding me at all. I feel like with every blink the inches of me expand like dough.

"Who the fuck is the Kardashian clan?"

I laugh out loud, but when I look at Stella's frown, I realise she genuinely doesn't know. The relief is so overwhelming I laugh even harder, so hard I shake. When I finally calm down, Stella is watching me intently, bemused. I stare back, but I can feel the laughter tease inside me—her lips are twitching, too, and we burst out laughing. The joke has changed though; it's no longer about the Kardashians and stretch marks, it's about the two of us, our differences from each other and from everyone else. We are different in so many aspects, but our curiosity in each other is the same. She leans on me to catch her breath as our giggles fade, reappearing like hiccups until we settle into silence.

Stella stands in front of me, a good few inches taller and several inches narrower. Gently, her fingers reach out to my stomach and retrace the scar. I almost feel the slice anew, caught at the point of escape and left dangling between. Between what, this time, is hard to say. Between the solid, unshakeable memory of David and the substantial surrealism of Stella. Her hands slide to my hips, warm and soft, but it's her eyes that I feel the most. They don't hurt me.

She kisses my lips. "What's wrong with your body?" she asks again, and this time I understand.

*

It must be nearly dawn. There is quiet now, settling in like dust. Stella's bedroom is filled with the smell of the bonfire smoke and, somewhere, her perfume. We are both naked under her blankets. I am acutely aware of the sameness and the difference of our bodies. Our hands are locked—gently though, like the threading of a bow through a child's hair. Her fingers are longer than mine, and my palm is a little broader. Stella kisses my shoulder, turns to her side. Her head finds the crook of my neck, and so do her lips. Our hands drift, follow the patterns of our bodies. This time, I find her mouth first.

10

Morning. I open the window for some air. Spring rain douses the last tendrils of smoke from the blackened earth of the bonfire outside. Stella tiptoes behind me and leans over the windowsill, still naked, and shouts good morning greetings to her relatives as they shout back from their caravan doors. In the daylight I am less sure of my body, suddenly unfamiliar with it, and I retreat to the bed again as if cold. I cling to the blankets as some sort of limp armour.

"You're going to tell me you're all naturists or something, aren't you? Well I won't be going out there, stark naked, I'm telling you now," I say, trying to make light of my discomfort, which I am sure she will notice. I am convinced that she sees me without even looking.

Stella laughs and glances over her shoulder. "No, we're witches, like Arthur said..."

"I can believe that."

She throws herself atop the bed. "It's true. That raven on Alma's hat is her familiar, Edgar. Milton is my familiar."

"I never knew happy, slobbery dogs could be witches' familiars."

She laughs again. "Does seem strange. I should have a

toad or something. Or maybe that cat that lurks in the barn."

"What is with Alma's weird hat, anyway? It looks bloody ridiculous."

The laughter in Stella's voice drifts away, though she still smiles at me. "It *is* Alma's familiar, in a way. She had a row with Arthur and her grandfather as a teen, about going to university or staying to work the farm. In a temper she hurled a stone across the field and hit the raven. Poor thing couldn't fly after. She put it in a box in the barn to keep it safe while it healed." She looks at me. "She went to visit uni the next day, took Arthur's car without permission. He found the raven and shot it."

"What?"

Stella shrugs, but doesn't seem truly nonchalant. There's anger in her voice. "Yep. She didn't say a word about it, just took it to a taxidermist in secret, made the hat. Whenever she had to stay on the farm, she wore the hat. No less than a month later, Arthur's cattle got foot-and-mouth, a totally isolated outbreak, and Arthur couldn't afford to run the farm fully operational after that. Alma had to deal with the mess, but Sybil managed to go to uni. So Alma is convinced it's her lucky talisman."

"I get why she made it taxidermy. But why a hat? Must be heavy."

Stella shrugs. "He had his flat cap. I suppose she wanted to outmatch him. He really did think of it as a crown—the sign that he was in charge of the farm, in charge of everyone and everything in it."

I nod. I think of David's possessions that remain in a box

in the back of my wardrobe at the flat, the things he has forgotten about. I've been keeping them for the day he might suddenly need them, might need me, and pop up at my doorstep with the flowers he never once bought me—but of course he would then, because he had finally realised he needs me like I needed him to need me. Stupid. He won't miss the second set of car keys, the bottle opener-torch combo my mum proudly presented to him for Christmas our first year together, the novelty underpants in the shape of an elephant trunk I bought him for Valentine's on a whim, an empty wallet, the wad of letter-headed paper he never used, his favourite mug for coffee, a pair of ankle weights, an Oasis CD, and several odd socks. Even though they are in a box, out of sight, they seem to invade my space, cluttering my flat as if he owns it. A king in his own home doesn't need a crown. He just lives in the brick and mortar, the same way David's voice lives in my head. I look at the bare walls of Stella's room, wondering if Arthur is still there, watching. Did he watch us in bed together last night?

We lie side by side, face to face. I put my hand on her arm. "I'm sorry, Stella. I'm sorry your granddad was so horrible."

She peers at me. "How do you mourn the loss of someone you hate?"

My answer is to kiss her. "This... accident that they mentioned yesterday. What happened?"

She takes a deep breath. "It was my eighteenth birthday. Some of my family blame me. Like I know they blame me for the fire at the nursing home."

"What—why?"

She taps the tattoo on her neck. "This symbol means fire. I got it on my birthday—booked it in with a friend, right at midnight. Arthur always hated tattoos, and I knew it. It's why I wanted one so badly. I especially wanted something to do with fire, because of the fire in the thirties that had nearly killed Arthur's granddad."

So, this is what happened: sometime between midnight and 2 a.m., while Stella was getting her tattoo, Arthur realised his granddaughter wasn't at home. He had a habit of spying on her through the slit of her bedroom door, which she wasn't allowed to get a lock on, to check she hadn't run off in the night (she had a habit of running off in the night). He thundered round the house, banging on all the doors, shouting, *Out, out, out! She's gone out!* Woke up Alma and Sybil, who did what they could to pacify him. Nothing soothed him so well as brandy, so as he stormed up and down the house, he drank until he smashed the bottle against the wall and rounded on Sybil. She always knew what Stella was up to, always kept her secrets. Alma got between them, as she always did. But by then, Stella was parking up outside. She could see that the lights of the house were on, and through an open window she could hear Alma and Arthur shout obscenities at each other. So she raced inside to take aim herself, or otherwise take the place of her aunts as his target. They were at the top of the stairs. His whole body was shaking with rage like she'd never seen before, and he was demanding she respect the rules of his house while she was under his roof, and that meant that she couldn't skulk off like a common tart to fuck whoever she pleased. He swung for her; she ducked; he missed, and he fell down the stairs, hit his head on the bottom bannister, and suffered a minor stroke.

I hardly know what to say and tell her as much. Instead I pull her close to me, and kiss her neck, on the tattoo. "There's no way that was your fault."

She hums, uncertain. "But when you wish for something so badly, and it happens, do you not at least feel a little guilty?"

"As in, 'be careful what you wish for', d'you mean?"

Stella nods. "I told him I wished he were dead. That all of us did. And that's what made him swing for me—what made him fall."

"Nah, it can't be that," I say. "After all, you said you wanted him to die, not fall over and have a stroke."

She chuckles, just a little. For a moment we take comfort knowing that our wishes don't have power. Or perhaps we regret that they don't. "Anyway," Stella begins, smiling brightly again. "You should shower. I'll get you a brew. I should warn you—we only have herbal decaff blends."

She shows me to the bathroom down the landing and hands me a towel so I can wash away the smoke from my hair and skin. The bathroom is the size of a cupboard and I can't help but think that's what it must have been, once. I tug on the chain to turn on the light bulb, which swings from a low ceiling just above my head. The shower is in a small cubical, affixed half-way up the jagged tile wall at shoulder height. I wonder how on earth Stella could possibly manage—or Arthur, when he had lived here. Despite the awkward manoeuvring of my body, the water is warm and falls heavily on my skin. The water runs a little red, the colour of my hair dye, but I like to think of it as if I'm bleeding out David.

I haven't showered this frequently in months. I lather up the soap over my body, wondering what Stella sees in me, what she felt. My thighs chafe, my breasts resent bras, my pubic hair—well, it grows. *What's wrong with your body?* David could tell her, but I know she wouldn't listen. I don't want to listen, either. The sounds that fill my head instead are the sounds from yesterday: the crackle of the bonfire, our laughter, our kisses.

My first time with David had not been so at ease, and definitely with less mutual satisfaction. In fact, nor had any of my first encounters with men, especially not *the* first time. I'd always put that down to the usual teenage state of things—the fumbling awkwardness of it all. I don't remember the feeling of it, just the setting, as if a page from a book somebody else had written: we were drunk, but prepared—he with a condom, me freshly shaven, makeup applied, wearing sexy and uncomfortable underwear underneath a carefully selected outfit, body perfumed and lotioned.

Some months ago, I'd bought a pack of condoms for myself for the first time in a bid to take charge of fuck knows what precisely, feeling like a feminist. But reflecting now on how much I had to do just to be *sex-body-ready*, aside from simply having a body of my very own, I reckon it's still the man's job to buy protection: he has fuck all else to do.

That very first time, though, my boyfriend had nicked a

condom from his older brother. Two of his mates waited for us outside the house, smoking, while we attempted to lose our virginity in the living room. That was when I noticed that goldfish pick up those little stones at the bottom of the tank and spit them out against the glass, seeking either escape or suicide. After my boyfriend had managed it, the lads came in and played video games while I sat texting my friends.

After my shower, I step outside and pick up the towel, which I'd left on a tiny stool—an old milkmaid's stool, I like to think. I wrap it around me, but then I notice: there's a flat cap there. I freeze. The second one that's been in the house. There's an itchiness crawling up my spine and spreading across my shoulders, weighing me down. Whenever Arthur thought he'd lost it, I helped him find it. I can't help but think the same is happening now; that his dark eyes have multiplied, spider-like, and spy throughout the numerous cracks in the old woodwork to catch the thief. And here I am, the faithful servant, finding it in plain sight again. I pick it up, careful in case I find it is nothing more than tissue paper that will melt away under my damp fingertips. It isn't. It's coarse, sturdy. I turn it over in my hands, bending it in the middle, testing the rigidity of the brim, looking inside and out as if I might find Arthur hiding in the folds, small and shrunken, an insect.

"Hey, Stella," I say, stepping out of the bathroom and padding to her bedroom. "Just how many flat caps did Arthur have?"

She's combing her hair in front of the long mirror beside the window. Incense is smoking on the sill, beside two cups of steaming tea. "Only the one."

I hesitate, the flat cap in my hands. I feel nervous, remembering that Sybil had already secretly burnt one in the pyre. "I found another."

"What do you mean?" she says, turning to face me. Her eyes settle on the flat cap. Stella snatches it out of my hands, muttering something below her breath, and launches it like a frisbee out of the window.

I look over her shoulder to see where it landed: just outside the damp ring of flower-mulch that surrounds the charred ground. The women below, huddled with hot drinks in the doorways of their caravans, look up in surprise. Hazel, wearing a dark tartan skirt that trails along the muddy ground, leaps forward and strides toward the house. The scruffy mongrel begins to bark, a deeper, gruffer sound than I had expected of the little thing who had spent the better part of the day before stealing sausage rolls and falling asleep. Hazel stops to follow the direction of his anger. Stella leans further out the window, looking sharply to the left. I stand beside her, leaning further over the window to see what the fuss is about.

A sleek black BMW has parked on the gravel beside mine at the gate. A suited man emerges, carrying a briefcase. I recoil: I see David in the suit and tie, the brown hair combed neatly forward. Though, of course, he has a Nissan, and a beard. The man who is not-David offers his hand to Hazel, but she folds her arms across her chest and turns away. He scurries to keep up with her stride and dodge the dog yipping at his ankles.

"Fuck," Stella whispers.

"Who is it?"
"The solicitor."

11

The first guy I dated—properly, not in the schoolgirl way you'd giddily agree to be someone's girlfriend just because they asked without even a date or a slobbery kiss first, had been on a training contract. I was in my final year at uni, and he'd finished his degree five years earlier, but still had a habit of drinking on Student Tuesdays in Leeds. We met in some hipster gin club, arms leaning on the sticky surface of the bar, elbowing each other to shout our order first, before the bar staff locked eyes with someone else and forgot us. I ordered my customary vodka coke, and he ordered a vodka tonic at the same time. It used to be our story: the way we bonded over a mutual dislike for the sudden popularity for gin when vodka was so much better. After we'd fucked on his blow-up mattress later that night in the house he had been renting for two years, he'd asked me how many times I'd cum. Not the traditional *if* I had: how many. None, obviously. This had never happened to him before, apparently. When I left him five months later, this became the story I told my girlfriends over a glass of wine at the local, we each rolling our eyes and slamming our drinks down, indignant.

I baked two parkins when I left him and ate nothing else

until they were gone. One for the end of our relationship, and one for the busted lip he'd given me. I never did tell my friends, or sister, or anyone, about that.

I want to tell Stella about him. About the first boyfriend, finding him on the park bench with Jenny. About hasty, hateful hand jobs behind bins. About scoring a six on the uni group chat, whereas Rachel with the weirdly long neck got a nine. About David's jigsaw body. How eager and clumsy his hands were, trying to smooth me away, whereas my hands, always curious, wanted to find a curve somewhere, a dimple, even.

I lie flat on my back and stare up at the sloping ceiling. I wonder what he would think, knowing I had felt the warmth of Stella's body sink into mine, how the sweet scent of bonfire smoke blended with the smell of our sex. Possibly, he would decide that this explained everything— though what that *everything* was would be inexplicable to him: the most important thing being that he would feel absolved from some accidental sin. That was always the way of it: original sin for us women, Eve's deliberate bite, while men always bite with their eyes shut.

I feel hungry. I think of biscuits, and Arthur. Is he in the ceiling, watching me? Stella said he used to spy on her. There's a crack, like a thin strip of lightning, across the wooden beam. Where the lines cross, an eyelet looks back at me, unblinking.

I have had enough of lying around and doing nothing. I want to see Stella, but this time I know the solicitor is here on strictly family business, and I am the guest. I do not think of myself as a stranger anymore, though perhaps I am a stranger to myself, like I have shed my skin, as if Stella has peeled me like an orange.

Wrapping a cardigan around my shoulders—one that Sybil left me last night, in case I found it chilly—I step into the landing again, and peer down the bannister. Maybe this is the staircase Arthur fell down, after he'd tried to slap Stella. From up here, I try to listen to their conversation in the living room. Faint mumbles and the whiff of coffee is all I get from this vantage point. I creep down a few steps, wincing as they creak under my feet. The most I get is the tone: Alma's voice is clipped and nettled, and even Sybil sounds piqued. I don't hear Stella.

I remember the night I had found David with his student. I had opened the front door, my front door, with my key, and stepped onto my mat, took my shoes off—heard a giggle. It cut through the air and slapped me. I shrank back against the wall, looking at the stairs, the coat rail, the mirror. That voice didn't belong to me, and therefore these things didn't, and yet it was all so familiar. I pressed my ear against the living room door, listening to that voice that was not mine. I remember trembling. I had asked him, hadn't I—I had asked him if he was having an affair. It would explain why he was so suddenly attached to his phone, why my face was no longer the background photo, but some stock image of a seaside. It explained things I couldn't articulate, things that if I said aloud would sound foolish—things he would laugh at.

I am doing much the same now, sneaking further down the curling staircase while I bite my lip at every creak. But I don't feel like a stranger. I am welcome here. I have shared

Stella's bed. It is Arthur's presence that needs to be dispelled. That is why the solicitor is here: there is something wrong with the will. He has done something clever, something spiteful. He probably wants his fucking flat cap back.

The murmur of voices takes shape, and I hear snatches of solid words.

"That doesn't make any sense," Stella says.

"I'm afraid, Ms Shipton, it is quite clear. The farm can only be inherited by a male heir, as it always has been." The solicitor sounds like a smug bastard, if you ask me.

"Totally absurd," Alma retorts. "That sort of nonsense can't be legal anymore."

"What does that mean?" Sybil asks.

There's a thud of someone's fist punching a couch or pillow. "I don't want to hear any more of this." Stella's voice. "Besides, there aren't any men in the family."

There is an uncomfortable cough from the solicitor. "Well, ma'am. In cases like this, we do have to conduct an investigation to ensure the will is properly fulfilled."

"Fuck that," she spat back, but the solicitor went on: "We have found that there is an illegitimate male child who stands to inherit the farm." He pauses, and I hear the ruffle of papers as he reviews his investigation. "Ah, here—Professor Fenton, an esteemed lecturer from Leeds."

Heat surges through me, circling in my head, angry wasps. *Out, out, out—get out of my house.* I fall forward into the door, bursting upon their discussion, and land heavily on my knees.

Stella rushes to me, though I don't recall even noticing

her approach. She's brushed my hair off my face, her expression flitting between concern for me to fury at the solicitor whenever she looks back at him. She, of course, doesn't know Professor Fenton is David. (Well, he's not Professor, not yet, but I have no doubt he'd let that slide.) She thinks I'm just hungover, no doubt, and need to soak up last night's alcohol.

Sybil fusses over me too, muttering *oh dear, oh dear*, and fetches water. Alma declares it is the end of the meeting and demands the solicitor takes his leave, but he frets about how to make an appointment as they have neither telephone nor email.

"We'll find you, don't worry," she says. The threatening tone in her voice demands his silence.

The solicitor is almost pushed through the kitchen and outside, eagerly thrust into the rain by Alma's bony fingers. Stella has looped her arm through mine, but she is rigid again, eyes fixed on the solicitor's back as I shuffle with them. Sybil maintains her welcome smile, but the clutch of her skirt in her fists speaks loudly of tension.

The rain is sprinkling now, but we venture outside. The mongrel is growling at the man, hackles up, as if the little scruffy thing were a Rottweiler. Milton joins too, bounding out of the barn doorway where he had been taking shelter, to prowl beside Stella, keeping low to the ground as if he, the slobbery spaniel, will make an attack. The solicitor, though, pauses to say goodbye to the Shipton women, promising to be in touch soon. Professional to the last, and fake to boot. Hazel, and Matilda, and Viv, and the other women, are slowly emerging from the caravans, long loose hair defying the rain. Their eyes never leave him. Nor do mine. They are all silent, and so my mouth is shut. We step forward onto the mud, our bare feet sinking slightly into the ground, our toes curling around tufts of wet grass. *Ours.*

The solicitor turns to face Alma and Sybil. Hazel approaches him from behind. "I am sorry, madam, but there is not much I can do." The women have made a circle. The solicitor stands in the middle, increasingly bewildered. The wind whips up, and I can see his fingers tighten around his briefcase as it batters against his knee. He passes Arthur's flat cap on the ground, sodden now, and limp. He hesitates and cocks his head, as if listening to a whisper. He bends down and picks up the hat, slaps off fresh rain drops. He puts it on his head.

Hss. The rain begins to pour, as heavy as it did when I was in Haworth, trying to find Goblin Market. I remember then what Nadiya had said about the rain being Arthur trying to put the fire out. I wasn't so sure he wasn't actually trying to drown us.

The solicitor backs away, one hand on his head to keep the flat cap steady. "Listen now, ladies—there's no need to shoot the messenger." His face has fallen white. His fingers toy with the hat. Why he's claimed it, I don't know. But it doesn't feel right.

Hss. Lips part, tongues slide between teeth, lungs empty air: the women are hissing. Viv started it, a tremulous, spiteful, half-whistle, as she glowers at the man. She points her finger at the solicitor. "You're nothing but a snake." Hazel mimics her noise, and so, of course, Alma does too. Soon they are all hissing, chasing the snake with the lashing of his own serpentine language. There is so much anger it is stifling.

Stella takes my hand, clings to me, and hisses.

Hss. The sound that I make, so hot with ire my throat is burning.

The solicitor throws off the flat cap and runs to his car.

Until his BMW disappears from view, we make that sound. As he shrinks, we drop to a whisper, and my certainty that this is a good thing to do—that this is a totally normal thing to do—falters. Stella has a firm grip on my hand and I am solid, whole. The solicitor has gone.

But David is circling my head like a vulture. He's up there, above Stella too, above the house.

12

It's Friday. It's fucking Friday. I've been so swept up in the farm, and Stella, and that weird hissing ritual, I'd almost forgotten. But the unexpected revelation that David is due to inherit Shipton Farm—David the sports-scientist, who only tolerates mud when on a rugby pitch—overwhelms me like a horse's back leg has kicked me, right in my gut.

I vomit in a bush. Well, over it. A spew of yellow bile and whatever I ate yesterday. I could die from embarrassment as Stella holds my hair and rubs my back. It is only when I have caught my breath and been forced to a seat inside that I am able to muster an explanation. Stella gives me another cup of herbal tea, promising it will settle my stomach.

When I tell them that Professor Fenton is my ex-husband, my unofficially divorced spouse, my daily torment, they are not at all surprised.

"Fancy that, Sybil," Alma says with a sniff.

She nods enthusiastically. "Quite a coincidence, indeed."

Coincidences always freak me out. This one is unsettling, but I can't explain why. I have run out of words. I've run out of memories. I think about why I am there. Why I went to the funeral, why I went to find Goblin Market. Why did I hiss at a solicitor with a bunch of women

I met only yesterday? I have not just run out of words; I have run out of pretence, or whatever it is that compelled me to simply go along with all this, to draw me in like the tide. Maybe I've finally come up for air.

"What am I doing here?" I say quietly, staring down at the tea cup. Stella tenses. I look at her, uncertain if she is a stranger or a lover or something entirely different. "What am I doing here?" I ask again, much more firmly.

Sybil turns to answer me, eyes bright and cheeks flushed. "You were kind enough to pay your respects to my late father, and to bring Alma and I over here in your car. We invited you to stay. Indeed, you were keen to stay."

I shake my head. "But why did—why did I even go to Haworth, to Goblin Market?"

Stella is still silent. Sybil rushes to respond. "Oh, how lovely! You didn't say you went to visit our little shop. No doubt Nadiya persuaded you to buy that necklace. It's her favourite, you see."

I shake my head so much I wonder if my brain will rattle against my skull like a pea in a pot. And that is about the size of my brain, I think—a bloody pea. What have I been doing this week? Chasing utter nonsense. Maybe the sugar has softened my mind too much; maybe now I am made so much of sugar, I might dissolve.

"I found matches with the flowers at the nursing home," I say, watching Stella's face for any sign of... well, anything. Confusion, admission, indignation. She remains blank. Her beautiful dark eyes with their dance of mischief doesn't give anything away. "Where was Arthur's body cremated?"

Finally Stella reacts: she huffs, folding her arms across

her chest. "You should know. You were there."

"But I don't think I *do* know." I rise, deciding in that moment that I have to leave. I have to get out. I have to go home. I have to go for drinks with David and his cronies. I have to go back to normal life, even if my life is a shambles; back to the couch, to the swell of memories pressing down on my chest, to the smell of ginger and sugar. I can almost taste the parkin on my tongue, tacky and sweet.

Stella does not stop me. She just follows me through the house while I gather my things, a reluctant shadow. I wonder if she is sad. I think I am, a little. But I don't know why. Maybe it is just all the wine from the night before, swirling up a noxious mix of feelings that have been buried under sugary-sludge for over a year. Maybe they have been buried for far longer.

Outside, heading for my car, all the women are busy dismantling the remains of the pyre. They don't notice me, or perhaps deliberately ignore me, which is just as well, as I don't feel like saying goodbye. Goodbye is too familiar, too close to needing a hug. Sybil is with Alma, raking up the ash, shooing away the curious cat as it searches for heat. Stella says nothing, does nothing, just watches me. I can feel her eyes on my back as I climb into the car, itching between my shoulder blades.

I remember when I first saw her on *Look North*, how perfect she seemed when I paused the television, her hair ruffled by the breeze, exposing the sparkle of her piercings around her ear. That little tattoo on the nape of her neck, the tattoo I had kissed, where I had inhaled the scent of her hair and the faint smoke upon her skin.

I turn the key in the ignition. Time for the daydream to be over. At least I was real, for a while.

13

I found an old bottle of perfume under the bed but I've put too much on. David doesn't like that. I don't suppose anybody does. I missed my neck with the last squirt, too, and now it's all on my tongue. Tastes foul.

I've rummaged around in my wardrobe for at least two hours in the hope to find something that says, with subtle pride, *I'm well, thank you, just look at me shine.* I fancy a little sprinkle of afterglow still radiates in my flushed cheeks, but that's probably just my overzealous dusting of blusher. A pair of leggings and a long mesh top with a deep-v cut will have to be good enough, especially with tummy-tuck pants on underneath and a plunge bra with cups the size of fucking craters.

The Uber guy swears he's taken the quickest route, but we both know there isn't a quick route to Leeds on a Friday night. It hums, everywhere, like a hive of bees drunk on nectar. There are groups of lads in football shirts, already blurting a rousing chorus of "Mr. Brightside" as they meander across the road without checking for cars. My driver pounds his horn, calling them *animals*. The weekly hen party is just beginning; the neon-clad brood happily waves inflatable penises at grim-faced bouncers. The swarm descended early this Friday. My taxi inches sluggishly forward; eventually the driver reckons I'd be better off walking the rest of the way, to which I simply agree even though I know I'll struggle to move any faster while swerving the heels of my boots away from the crevices between the cobblestones.

By the time I'm outside Hop Scotch, I'm flushed and sweaty, wondering how early perimenopause can kick in, figuring it'd be just my luck to start in my early thirties. Hovering outside, I try to catch my breath, dabbing at the stubborn sweat swamping my forehead with a sleeve. A meek little squeak inside says I shouldn't be here, I've got it wrong, I've always got it wrong. I am wrong.

I feel more out of place than ever, less myself than ever. I like the backstreets, the indie cafes, the shops with random junk and old trinkets nobody ever really wants until you look at it in just the right light, or turn it over in your palms just the right number of times. I don't like this white noise, the sameness of it all, where all the women are variations of the same doll, all the men the same variation of blazer and soft beard. The monotonous Mondays and months and modern life.

But I've assembled myself; I resemble Kat, vaguely. I've settled on being a brave new kind of woman, the woman who doesn't need to eat a whole cake in one sitting just to smoke out her soon-to-be ex-husband from the warren he's burrowed into her brain. The kind of woman who can congratulate her ex-husband on his promotion and demand a divorce.

With a gulp of air held tight inside my lungs, I push open

the door. The standard pub anthem of limp rock—that nasal drawl David loves so much—slaps my ears, and the heatwave of crowded bodies flushes my cheeks instantly. I feel nauseous. My tongue is dry and my throat is hot, like I've swallowed a spoonful of cinnamon. Squirming my way through the maze of people, I'm painfully conscious of how much my body is squeezed and pressed between so many strangers, out of control. Am I swelling? No, just sweating.

What's wrong with your body? Stella says; I can even hear the gentle smile in her words. It's comforting.

That's when I find David, at the back, in his favourite spot. He's always the life of the party when it's his own; any other time, he grumbles and watches the time, pestering to leave. Tonight, he's laughing, telling his captive audience about his next five-year plan, drinking whiskey on the rocks.

A woman sits beside him. His hand is on her bare knee. But she is not the student he had an affair with. She's a little older than the student had been, though she's still under thirty. She's a pretty brunette, and never takes her eyes off him, never stops smiling. She's drunk in love. She's a bloody fool.

But then again, so am I.

"Oh god, Kat!" David exclaims before I am ready to face him, to wield my words. "I didn't know you'd be coming tonight." He does not stand up to greet me, but he grins, clearly already half-cut, as he rubs his hand along the length of the leg of his new woman.

I force a smile. "Was I supposed to RSVP or something?"

"No, but—oh fuck, I sent you the group text, didn't I? I'm

so sorry!"

My stomach drops so low it may well have tumbled out of me. I'm not supposed to be here. I'm not invited. It's just a mistake. Everyone is staring at me. Some of the faces around me are familiar, ex-colleagues who still believe our divorce was a mutual, amicable decision, that we had simply fallen out of love, like people do.

And yet. David doesn't have much social tact, I know that—but there's a smirk on his face that unsettles me. Maybe this is a test, a deliberate mockery. Is it Arthur's smile I see in him now? The silence stretches while I study his jawline, his eyes, his stature. He does look like Arthur, I suppose. It's in his height, the shape of his face. I can't help but wonder if he's the new devil, if he's inherited Arthur's title as well as the deeds to his property.

I clear my throat and take a deep breath. "Well, you were always shit at communicating!" I force a laugh, and some of his guests chuckle awkwardly. "I'm here now, so I may as well get a few drinks." That is about as brave as I can be.

*

It's something like 1 a.m. Wait, maybe earlier. Or later. I'm really drunk. Call it sometime between midnight and 2 a.m. David's ex—not me, I am THE ex, the ex-wife, the mistake. But not a baby mistake. Obviously. Losing track now.

David's ex, the student one, shows up. She clearly doesn't do my cake trick after a break up; she's skinnier than ever, hollowed out around the eyes, chiselled through the cheeks. Funny, how much our bodies are carved and moulded by men. And she doesn't look like I remember her. Her tits are teeny, despite the efforts of her little black dress to enhance her cleavage. Her teeth are big and white and her lips are swollen like pink plastic slugs. Her makeup has become dirtied and patchy through long wear. Mascara and eyeliner, clumped and smudged, stain her happy-printed face with fat black raindrops.

I see her distress and realise: she's just a naive young woman. She doesn't know it yet, but she's had a narrow escape. She deserves better than David, just like I do. But it's worse for her. This should be her story, I suppose. She's the student, the doe-eyed young woman overawed by the lecturer, his intelligence, his casual wit, his charming smile. With the pressure of study and the promise of career on her shoulders, all while she's supposed to be light and fun and perfect, it's no wonder she followed his lead.

I should have reported David to HR. But how could I ruin him like that, all his hard work, his future? That's what he told me. It would be nothing but petty and spiteful if I did; I would ruin her prospects, too. And he so clearly cared for her. It's real love, you see, when you risk everything to fuck someone who is willing to ask *how wide?* whenever you tell them to open their mouth.

Now I understand why the Shipton women hissed at the solicitor. I want to bare my teeth and hiss at him until he is so full of terror he flees in wild panic, never to be seen again.

I think I am hissing, actually. Yes, I'm hissing, quietly, while I watch his other ex slam through the pub to confront him.

"You lying prick!" she shouts, her finger aggressively pointing in his direction as if to stab at every word. "I fucking hate you! I wish you were dead, you lying prick! You just needed some space, huh? Needed to focus on your promotion, right? Bullshit! You went straight on Tinder and started fucking around, didn't you?"

David rises calmly. I always hated how he could be so level-headed when other people were around, yet how much he could shout, how much he could smash, how much he could threaten the second we were alone. Much like his father, I presume.

Apologising to his company for the disruption, and giving a reassuring squeeze to his new girlfriend's shoulder, he approaches his ex and urges her outside, where they can talk privately. I follow them at a distance, a hiss still coiling on the tip of my tongue.

It's cool and quiet on the street. The other pubs are shut, windows black with shadow. There's just the three of us outside, only they don't notice me. For once, I want it to be this way. I want to be the forgotten ex-wife.

"You're drunk and embarrassing me as well as yourself. You should go home," David says in a low grumble. He slightly pushes her, and she totters backward in her heels. "Go home, Evie."

She staggers after him, tugging on his sleeve. "You won't answer my calls! Don't you think I deserve to know the truth? I dropped out of uni for you!"

David rolls his eyes. "I never *told* you to do that."

Her mouth hangs open, somewhere between

mortification and indignation. I remember that feeling well, only it was always humiliation that won out. Tears shine in her eyes. "Did you ever even care about me?"

He shrugs casually. Just a shrug. That's what she is worth to him—that's what our marriage was worth to him. I clench my fist, and the hiss rises in my throat.

She hiccups a sob, and hiccups again, trying to catch her breath. Her fingers claw at her chest as if to quell the thunder of her heart. "You absolute prick!" She charges at him, gives her all to push him backward. But her fury is not enough, and he merely laughs. "Don't you fucking laugh, you monster!" She tries to shove him again, and again, and again, each time driving him back but a step or two onto the road.

He remains unfazed while she slaps her hands upon his chest and cries, but the laughter in his voice turns bitter, irritated. He seizes her upper arms, looks her square in the face, and snarls, "Do you think I would ever love a silly little girl like you?"

They stand in the middle of the road, so close they would look like lovers in a romcom, but I see the hate and hurt that draws them together.

I hear the screech of wheels turning a corner, and the sudden frantic blare of a car horn. I'm drunk, very drunk, so I'm not sure what I'm doing or why. But I know I lurch forward, taking them both by surprise, and I separate David from his ex-lover. I remember the heat of my palm upon his chest. I remember the wetness of her wrist under my grip; she'd just wiped her snotty-tears from her face along her arm. I hear the rev of the engine, the shudder of the car straining to halt.

I hear the thud and clunk of David slamming into the bonnet, rolling over the top, the thump of his body as he hits the ground. Evie screams. I run down the street, laughing.

14

I spend the next morning baking three parkins.

Stirring is always satisfying to me, and the smell of treacle remind me of my grandma's kitchen, and of her colour-coordinated clothes, the Wool Queen of Bradford. Of my mother, too, trying to bake parkin herself when I was a young teen, for grandma's wake. To this day I have no idea what the hell went wrong with her batch. She had warned me that my grandma had written the instructions incorrectly, likely on purpose, so that it would come out tasting rancid and burnt. But I had been baking with her for a few years as a kid. The first time I tried to bake it by myself was when I came back from seeing my first boyfriend fumble with Jenny on the park bench and went off to give Jenny's older brother a hand job behind the bins for a bottle of vodka. I remember thinking, *This is how to get Jenny to notice me.* I went home and made parkin and ate the lot, ate until the cake had gone and I had gone along with it.

My sister and mum both ring me, over and over, but I don't answer. They leave voicemails I don't listen to. My sister sends a message: *David was in a hit and run. He's at St James's Hospital. Doesn't look good. Mum thinks you should go see*

him but it's entirely up to you. I'll take you if you do want to go X.
I know exactly where I want to go.

*

Shipton Farm is busy. The geese are running riot, honking in protest whenever someone approaches to usher them back into their pen. The dogs try to assist, but they are no match for the stubborn ferocity of geese. Hazel oversees it all with a sharp eye while never herself drawing near. Matilda, in the centre, fusses with mud to hide the last phantom trace of the pyre. Alma points at any spot she has missed.

"Hello, dear," Sybil says, beaming as she approaches me. "What a pleasure to see you again."

"I hope you don't mind. I wanted to show my appreciation for your hospitality the other day, since I didn't say goodbye properly." I present the three large cake tins with a smile.

She clasps her hands in delight. "Your famous parkin! What a treat."

I don't remember telling her anything about baking, but I was fairly drunk at the wake. And last night. I want to tell Stella about last night. "Is Stella…?"

"Yes, yes, of course—she is in her room. Go right in."

She's braiding her hair. She is as beautiful as ever—more than ever, I think, and I let myself acknowledge it: acknowledge this feeling that pulls me to her, the feeling that warms me inside. I stare at her, suddenly shy.

"You came back." It is not a question.

I nod, a little nervous she is upset. "I'm sorry I left. I'm sorry I accused you of..." Well, I'm still unsure what I had accused her of, or thought, at the time. Coincidences freak me out—but that was just all it was. A coincidence.

She takes a step closer, the ghost of a smile whispering on her lips. "Good. Because I never wished for the nursing home to burn down. I only wished to find someone to love."

I bit my lip. I've wished, all this time, to find myself again. Only there was no *again* about it. I've never been anything but someone else. David's wife.

"Did you get David to sign the divorce papers?" Stella asked.

My smile broadens—I can't help it. I don't know if I feel guilty about that, or if I should. "No. He was in a car accident."

Stella smiles back. "Fancy that."

"Fancy that," I reply.

And then we step forward together, hold hands a little tentatively, but kiss with gentle, tender, eagerness. We go to bed together, learning the shapes we have, the softness and the heat, the thin-white lines of the scars that make but do not define us.

*

Late in the evening, when the earth below Stella's bedroom window is finally purged of all traces of the pyre and of Arthur, we are summoned to the kitchen. The three cakes are in the centre of the old oak table, which everyone clambers to sit around. Alma sits at the head, but Hazel elbows her way round to the other end. Opposite Stella and I, it is quietly agreed Matilda should have a seat, for her services, and Viv, for her age. Sybil leans beside her sister, and the rest encircle the table. Milton settles at Stella's feet underneath, and the mongrel yips until one of the twins bends to pick him up and settle him on Viv's lap.

"Thank goodness," Viv says, patting her pot belly. She is thin, seemingly frail, but her belly pops out as if a twig has swallowed a pea. "I am so hungry I could eat a man whole."

"Good thing, too," Alma says. "Because that's what we're going to do."

"Indeed it is," Sybil replies, gesturing for us to take a seat. Stella sits beside me, her hand on my knee, while Sybil continues: "Eating parkin is Kat's own little ritual, as it were. We have some devils to exorcise, and a farm to claim. So let's try, shall we?"

"We may as well give it a go," Hazel replies with a sniff. "We've not much else to lose."

There is quiet agreement among the table. Stella squeezes my hand, beaming. I feel needed as much as wanted, in all the right ways. Me: Kat, widow of David Fenton, heir to Shipton Farm.

"Ready everyone?" Alma says. Her raven-hat turns about as she sharply looks around the room. Its eyes, pools of watchful ink, seem to blink in the flickering light from the ceiling. "Three, two—"

"One!" Hazel shouts.

Arms stretch out and hands spread, fingers curling like claws. They sink their nails into the cakes, brutalising clusters of parkin into their hands and palms. Eager mouths bite down and swallow; they suck the crumbs from their fingers with loudly smacking lips; they rake more and more morsels into their nails and use their teeth to scrape it out. Even Stella extends her arms, graceful and fierce, and chokes away clumps of cake. They murmur, and growl, and hiss, hunters at a banquet of bones, ripping apart limb after limb and lapping up the bloody mess with eager tongues.

I sit still. I wonder if it is now strangely rude of me not to shred the cake with my bare hands as they do. It is like the hissing. I can feel myself tugged in, the surge of frenzy infectious, the hunger savage. So I reach out, push my fingers into the moist body of the cake, wrapping around the centre, and snatch out the heart. I flatten my loaded palm against my lips and lick away the crumbling cake, the taste of parkin melting on my tongue.

We eat, until all that's left in the house is us.

Short Stories

Mother Magpie

She sits like they do in those old Hollywood monster films: on the car bonnet of her car, which is parked at the top of a hill. It could be anywhere, almost—anywhere but Cripton. Smoke curls from chimneys below, smudging the clouds. Scattered streetlamps wink. The curved silhouette of the village breaks the skyline like the jagged lower jaw of a Cheshire grin. This is where her mother lives—lived.

This is where her mother used to live. She flicks away the stub of her roll-up. Already she feels the urgent want of another, the want of something to pacify the scream tugging at her lips. Or is it a sob? Something thick and tacky, stuck in her throat. She fights the urge, and picks instead at the skin around her fingernails. It is time to go back, she knows. She can survive two nights, surely. She tells herself this as she jumps down from the bonnet and climbs back into the car. Though she turns the key in the ignition, she sits, staring out at the dark. That something thick and tacky, stuck in her throat, crawls up to her mouth. But it is not a scream after all. It's laughter that claws its way out. Only her mother could do this. Only her mother could make her go back there.

When she pulls up in front of the house, it's almost

midnight. Everything is still. She slings her backpack over her shoulder and slams the car door shut. If she must be here, she must make noise, as if she could startle the house awake.

Her key still works in the lock and the door peels open. There remains a cadaverous smell, sour and putrid, hanging in the air, the odorous phantom of her mother's body. She had been dead almost two weeks before she was found sternly upright in the armchair, bloated, slack-jawed, wide eyes cataract-white, waiting. The gin bottle had fallen from her grip, and her swollen hand had forced her brittle nails deep into the skin of her palm. The mortician prised open her fingers like the unveiling of a Venus flytrap, revealing an undigested mulch of paper that still read her daughter's name.

So, she is back at the house as if summoned by the crow-call of her mother's voice, wondering if her mother and her house are now made of the same stuff, if her skin has seeped into the fabric, if her bones have furrowed into the timber, if her blood has cemented the stone.

She flicks the nearest switch; the lights along the hallway shudder on. The dust is thick, and mould mottles the floral wallpaper. A love-sick bouquet. She sighs, dumping the backpack to the floor. No doubt the neighbours thought her wicked, to have left her mother alone in such an old house. She could only imagine the stories her mother had told them of the despicable, undaughterly crimes she must have committed in her life, swanning off to the south at seventeen like that, turning her back to her roots, leaving her mother alone in such an old house while it ran to seed.

Did she not know how much her mother had given up just to raise her—all the dreams she had left behind?

No matter the yawn of years that stretched between the last time that they had spoken, her mother would not have changed. Of this she was certain. Her mother's fingers had never pinched a glow into cherubim grins, nor tenderly smoothed wayward tears into the cushion of her thumb. Her fingers had twirled strands of hair around and around, tight as a noose, and tugged to rip the curls from her head while she slept. Then awake, blood beading across her throbbing scalp, her mother would look down through the glasses on the tip of her nose, eyes bright, and she'd say: *I told you not to leave the window open at night. That magpie got your hair again.*

She will open all the windows throughout the house. Simple spite has its comforts. Out the back, into the kitchen where the tap still drips, she leans over the sink to lift the latch and pushes open the little window. There is an unsavoury smell in this room—of boiled potatoes, as ever, and soured milk and old meat. The fridge must be broken. *Tap, tap, tap,* is the sole sound in the kitchen; outside, the rush of wind through the trees, the scream of a fox.

She passes by the living room, though its door is open, beckoning. She can picture her mother in the doorway, licking at the liquorice stuck in her teeth, gums blackened, lips purple-cold. That is the mother she remembers most; the mother with frayed hair stuck with knitting needles, wrapped in homemade shawls, appearing at doorways to watch silently. This is where she would put her foot out, like a child in a school corridor, aiming at shins and ankles.

Whenever she fell, her mother would scoop her up into a rib-crushing embrace, and remind her not to trip over her own feet.

The dining room has the largest windows in the house. Her mother had used the space as a makeshift art studio, though she only sold the odd few paintings at the village hall on market weekends. Over the years, her mother stopped painting entirely, using the room instead to write belligerent letters of complaint to the local council, to the butcher on the occasion he cut her Sunday pork joint a quarter of a kilogram lighter than requested, to her daughter when she moved away to find her father. She should never have given her mother the address. She thought she would be safe, trusting to the fact that her mother refused to leave Cripton, that London was almost another country in her mother's mind. But the letters had come weekly. As soon as she learnt that her father had died of drink-induced liver disease, she left London for Brighton, and never gave her mother the new address. For thirty-four years, she had been free, untouchable. But the dead have a strange pull, she's lately learnt.

When she turns the lights on, she sees just how much her mother had neglected the room: wayward webs are woven through the fixtures, greyed by the thick film of dust; green and black bruises of mould shroud the ceiling and crevices in the walls; moths have made feasts of the curtains. The old typewriter is pushed to the corner of the table, no longer pride of place as it was when she lived there. Instead, jars and mugs of murky water line up the middle, paint brushes festering inside them. She steps closer, wondering if her mother had returned to painting. She finds only slashes of black and blue, layer upon layer so that the paper curls at the edges.

She shrugs. If her mother had lost her mind, it was not a mind worth finding again.

Careful of the webs that lace the latches, she swings open the large windows, and they whine, old bones in old joints reluctant to stretch. Their moan of complaint is satisfying.

When she leaves the room, the hallway lights are off. She does not think much of this; the electric has never been stable, and she has shocked herself on plug sockets more than once. She flicks the switch again, but they remain unresponsive. She tries the light for upstairs. Tries again: it flickers. She thumps the wall, once, twice. Light swells and the bulb bursts; darkness returns, and—

thump thump

somewhere behind her.

She grips the bannister white-knuckle tight, holds her breath, but hears only the familiar whines of the house as the wind whistles through its secret broken places. That thick and tacky feeling, stuck in her throat, returns; more viscous than before, she can't swallow it down. Again, it's laughter that bursts through. She feels foolish, childish, realising the *thumps* must only have been the wind buffeting the kitchen window. Perhaps she should have arrived earlier in the day after all—but no, she could not bear the thought of the neighbours shuffling to the edge of their fences or peering over the bushes, muttering about how much of a disappointment she had turned out to be, the only little girl on their quiet little cul-de-sac in their quiet little village, the girl who thought herself too good for Tom Ford, the plumber's boy.

Their tutting fills her head, echoes of her mother's raucous notes. They prod sticks at her belly. *Full, full, but not with a baby.* They seize upon her wrists. Fourth left finger unworn, kissed at every angle by sunlight but not shaded by a ring, not starved by its umbilical cord.

She picks up her backpack and marches upstairs, stamping as loud as possible. The bathroom is on the right, above the kitchen. She tugs the light string, hoping but doubting—and it works, though the light hums like a beehive. The window, above the toilet, is almost painted shut, and resists her heavy-handed pushing. With a disgruntled sigh, she drops her backpack to the floor so that she can shove the window with more shoulder strength while she kneels on the toilet for more leverage. Finally, the window flings open; she falls backward, off balance, and slams down upon the tiled floor, her head striking her backpack. She shouts out in pain, hands instinctively cradling her lower back and hip while she bites down, hard, upon her lower lip to fight her tears.

The pain has shocked the breath right out of her. She rocks back and forth, sucking in air through clenched teeth. Tentatively, she shuffles around, wincing when she leans too heavily on her side. Her head throbs. Gripping the sink, she hauls herself up. The thick, tacky feeling swells again, and the taste of blood on her lip is bitter. She spits into the sink, recoils at the black-red sludge oozing down the porcelain basin. Salty sweetness, an unpleasant but potent potion, lingers on her tongue. She turns on the tap, scoops water into her hands and cups it to her mouth to wash away the taste.

Blinking the water out of her eyes, she looks up. The face that meets her in the mirror above the sink slaps her with fear: her mother's face, sour, austere, old. But when she blinks again, she sees it is only her own. Crow's feet have made their mark around her eyes and sunken into the corners of her mouth, too; her hair, thinned by the teeth of her mother's pinch as a child, thinning now with age, frays at the edges like old wool. Purple-black lips, pulling into a rictus grin. Too much like her mother.

And, as she limps from the bathroom, she walks like her, too.

Her mother's bedroom is at the end of the corridor. Her own childhood bedroom is to the right. The door is ajar, and gently swings back and forth, as if to wave hello. The air that wheezes through the crack is cold, carrying with it the sickly scent of lilies. When she opens the door and turns on the light, the room is as it was when she was a child: smothered in nauseating pink and white, a candy floss kaleidoscope, from wallpaper to ceiling to bedspread. Wilted lilies with broken necks sag over the pink crystal vase on the dressing table. The dolls she had never liked are lined up across the bed, leaning upon the pillows, ready to play *ten in the bed*, to smash their china smiles as they roll over and bang their heads, one by one.

The window is already wide open. No magpie in sight, of course. But she lingers in the doorway, as if as soon as she passed through the threshold the *caw* would call and a bird would make a nest of her hair. Or her mother would appear, not dead after all.

She forces herself to shake away the nonsense filling her head. The cold is bone-deep now, but she refuses to shut the windows. Rummaging through her backpack for an extra jumper, she finds her flask has leaked, the cap broken from her fall. Her clothes for the next two nights are soaked.

It is with the utmost reluctance she enters her mother's room and fetches one of her many hand-knitted cardigans. This one has a little pad and pen in one pocket, and tissues in the other. It could have been worse; there could have been a needle in the pocket, waiting to prick her finger. Or gummed liquorice sticks, tacky with fragments of wool and dead skin. The familiar itch of the wool promptly irritates her neck. Her mother felt much the same though never said so, choosing instead to suffer to save money, scratching when she thought nobody could see. Her mother's smell is deep within the fabric too, enveloping her in the musty scent—the sourness of unwashed skin, the sickly-sweet liquorice of her breath. Earthy grime.

There is no point trying to open this window; it is nailed shut. Even so, the thought of smashing it to smithereens is tempting. It would merely look like someone had ransacked the room, after all; clothes are left upon the carpet, books are strewn on the table, a glass lies on the floor beside the stain of red wine. The bed is unmade, the imprint of her mother's body sunken into the old mattress, one half of a coffin-mould—waiting for the lid.

thump thump
somewhere below.

The noise startles her but, again, she assumes it is only the kitchen window, or perhaps the dining room windows. She looks over her shoulder; the bathroom light shudders, straining. The window taps. Determined to keep the windows open, she limps her way downstairs once more, fumbling through the dark. Her hip is sore, her back is aching; she grips the bannister to steady herself along the way.

thump thump

The heartbeat of the house sneers at her uncertain steps. It is definitely the kitchen window. Perhaps she did not put the latch on properly. Though it has been more than three decades since she last stepped foot in the house, every floorboard creak, every crack in the wall, every step in the dark corridor is uncomfortably familiar to her. She does not need light to reach the kitchen, where the smells from the broken fridge seem stronger than before.

She reaffixes the window to the latch and the heartbeat is silenced, but the stretch over the sink jabs at her bruised hip. The pain floods up and down her body, spasms her back. Gritting her teeth, she rummages through the cupboards in search of medication, finding nothing but bottles of gin. Her fingers twitch. She needs something to relieve the pain, to get her through the night before she can face the village, the neighbours. The funeral.

Sighing heavily, she seizes upon a bottle, unscrews the cap, and gulps down the dry, bitter liquor. It makes her head swirl.

She knows she cannot make it back up the stairs to bed. Besides, she could not stomach the thought of the dolls' room, or her mother's room. Stiffly, with another eager swig, she makes her way to the living room.

The sight she faces confounds her. Painted on the wall, behind the armchair, is a large magpie, wings outstretched in flight. Its white breast is pristine, like un-trespassed snow, the black-blue feathers shimmering as if her own shaking breath ruffled each, one by one. She coils a finger around several strands of hair, pulling in despair. Her mother's final masterpiece.

With a handful of her own thinning hair falling through her fingers, scattering to the floor at the feet of the magpie in reluctant homage, she refuses to be perturbed. She will stop thinking of *her*. This house is her own now.

Sinking into the armchair where the phantom shape of a body nests, she swigs the gin from the bottle to wash away her thoughts. That itch in the back of her throat rises up again, around her neck, clawing its way through her throat and into her mouth; out bursts raucous laughter, tremulous and choking, and with it black liquorice sap. Only her mother could do this to her, leave her alone in the old house, alone to age under the shadow of the magpie. Stuffing the gin bottle in the side of the chair, she buries her hands into her pockets, plucking out the pen and notepad kept there. She scrawls her name on a piece of paper, and holds it tight in her fist, lest she forgets.

House Proud

They say most murderers return to the scene of the crime. Can't help themselves. Not to check they didn't leave anything incriminating behind, as they're either too cocky or too stupid to check. In my experience, it's to revel in glory. It's like you can inhale their last breath all over again and get, you know... excited. Bit disorientating though, when the blood's cleaned up, and the yellow tape's gone, and everything's been reset, as if nothing ever fucking happened.

Weirder when, a whole year later, someone you know quite well moves in, when the drama of the death has settled down and the place has been revamped. Not just weird, but aggravating. When I saw him tour the flat with the letting agent, I wanted to slap him. Most I could do was throw a stone at the window when he looked out, but he didn't notice me. He and the agent seemed to get along like a house on fire. He laughed a hell of a lot, and she giggled like a bloody teenager meeting their celebrity crush. He had that kind of charm, Billie did.

I knew Billie from my university days. You'd be able to take one look at him and guess his degree of choice: Business. You know the type: wears sunglasses all year round, shark smile shines with whitened teeth, volume permanently set to shout. He had swagger, and cheeky charm, carefully disguising all his red flags with the waft of his wallet. Daddy owns a car company, apparently. So Billie gets what Billie wants and Billie does what Billie wants too, whether that was a new pair of trainers or colonising tattoos. But you'd come to forgive the shitty lion on his shoulder, and the tribal wraps, and the dodgy Chinese characters which are meant to say something profound like *eye of the tiger*—when everyone secretly hopes it just means *wanker*—if he bought you and the girls a whole tree of pornstar martinis with a sprinkle of roofie dust.

Obviously I wasn't doing his degree, but it didn't really matter. Every girl on campus knew Billie, one way or another. That's why I told him to fuck off that night I saw him at Revolution before he could even say hi.

That was a good few years back. I think the last time I'd seen him was about a year ago, on my way back from a bad date. We spotted each other on opposite sides of the road, and that was it.

I cannot believe he bought this place with cash. I watched him fetch a briefcase from the boot of his car like a drug dealer—which I wouldn't put past him—and show it off to the letting agent. I don't know what they said, but there seemed to be some reluctance on her part, until he stuffed a wad of cash into the pocket of her blazer.

I knew she'd come back too. She'd be uncertain if she should but excited by the thought even so. Stupid bitch. I was right, of course; she personally handed over the keys a week later when the paperwork was finalised and followed him in. She made some pretence about checking he was absolutely sure he wanted the flat, since... Her voice trailed off, unable to mention the murder. He fed her some bullshit about knowing the victim; not well enough to be too cut up about it, but well enough to feel a fondness for the flat that didn't touch grief. As if he ever shed a tear for anyone. Besides, he wasn't superstitious. She asked if he had visited the place frequently. He said he'd only been over that one time.

The rooms were all empty, but that didn't stop him from bending her over the kitchen counter. I looked down on them from the vent above, disgusted. Billie had no right.

He made the place a total bachelor pad. Charcoal coloured shit everywhere, black wood, whiskey in the wine rack. Bastard put up Pornhub posters, of all things. Before, there'd been decent art. Mucha's *The Seasons*, right over the bed. Beautiful art decor patterns and prints to match. A paradise of 1920s elegance in the shitty 2020s.

At night I got a proper look at his stuff while he slept. Opened the kitchen drawers to check the mismatched cutlery, likely squirrelled away from his old university digs or something. Mugs with stupid slogans and naff cartoons, the cheap gifts guys get for birthdays. His plates were square—square! And he didn't keep up with the washing. He kept the spoons overturned on the drying rack, so they got those white circles on them and always looked unclean. Don't even get me started on the bathroom. I refused to go in there.

Made me seethe, to see the once lovely little flat turned to this... grey blur of blandness. What was the point? He should have just stayed with his parents until he acquired some semblance of taste or inherited theirs. It infuriated me, to think someone should lose their life, and then for all their personality, their carefully curated lifestyle, to be wiped away by some walking male stereotype. Bloody business blokes.

Billie needs to know he can't just take what he wants. Just because he bought this flat, does not mean he owns it. He can't get rid of me so easily. So I decided to fuck with him. Just little things, at first. Like turning over the fucking spoons. But then I decided it would be far too helpful, and he just wasn't observant enough to notice.

I left a drawer open overnight. I knew the flat inside out, and I knew his habits by then too, so it was easy enough to watch him through the crack in the door, which he never shut. Rumour had it, back home with his parents, a maid did all the cleaning—I reckon someone else was hired to follow him around the house just to shut the bloody doors behind him.

In the morning he shuffled into the kitchen in his old jogging bottoms, shirtless, rubbing the sleep from his eyes. Did he notice the open drawer? Did he fuck. He just shut it with a flippant flick of his fingers.

I upped my game, piece by piece, to get under his skin. That one drawer turned into two. Then a cupboard door. It hurt to leave his cheap tat on display, but needs must. For a while he just shut them with a shrug. Slowly, after a couple of days, he started to feel nervous, I could tell. I watched him from above, out of sight. He started to pause in the kitchen, looking around, and when he closed the drawers he would tell himself, aloud, that he had shut them.

Time for more drastic measures.

When he left the room with his fresh coffee to go back to work in the office, I gently pushed open the vent and reached down, finding the top edge of the door he had left open yet again. I slammed it shut.

I scrambled to shut the vent again, nesting in position to watch him come running. He burst in, fist raised, ready to punch at the air. He circled round and round, demanding whoever the fuck was paying tricks on him to get out, or else. But there was nobody for him to find. I could hear him panting, outraged and anxious. I had to smother my mouth to stifle my laughter.

He backed out of the room, huffing, and closed the door behind him. Good. He was learning.

I let him get into work for about half an hour before I decided to unplug the Wi-Fi in the middle of a business call. He liked to think of himself as some sort of entrepreneur, a Lord Sugar kind of lad. If you've ever seen *The Apprentice*, you'll know they're all pricks, and Billie was no different. God, I hated listening to his sales calls. The schmoozing made me want to vomit.

I crawled through the vents on my belly between the kitchen to the living room. Old factory conversions have their benefits. I did my best to keep quiet—I had plans for much more noise later. One thing at a time. I slipped down, landing lightly on my feet in the living room. I unplugged the Wi-Fi on the socket below the ridiculously large television, which I sincerely wanted to batter with a cricket bat. It would take a short while for him to realise there was a problem, before he came in to check. Enough time to shuffle back up the vent.

As soon as he stomped into the living room and bent down to plug the Wi-Fi back in—I swear I saw him recoil when he noticed the leads had been removed from the port—I slammed the door shut behind him again.

He screamed and jumped round, staggering back into his television. I hadn't been quick enough; he'd seen my fingers tug the vent closed. But then the television behind him rocked on its mount with a whine, and by the time he tried to steady it, it was too late. The television fell from the wall and smashed on the floor.

Billie stood in the middle of his living room, swinging his gaze from his broken television to the vent, where I hid. He panted like a dog, fists clenched at his sides. But he was rooted to the spot, mouth hanging open like he was catching flies.

I decided now was the best opportunity to make full use of the vents. I flicked it open; he flinched, jumping back as it swung limply back and forth. I lowered my hand—just the hand—pointing my finger at him. I curled it slowly, beckoning.

"What the fuck? What the fuck?" he moaned hoarsely.

I shut the vent again, relishing the squeal of the hinge—sweet music to pair with his frightened swearing. This time I made no effort to keep quiet; I slapped my hands on the cold steel of the vent as I made my way across, settling in his bedroom. God, his bedspread was horrid. Plain grey. Even stripes are too much fun for Billie. Absolutely no personality or style. No brain cells either, probably.

Billie entered the room cautiously. "Becca? Is that you?" he whispered. So much for not being superstitious.

I retreated through the vents as quietly as I could this time. Let him think he'd lost his shit.

Back in the kitchen, I slipped out of the vent and opened all the drawers, still moving with stealth. I was pretty good at it by then—how long had I been in the flat, how many tours of would-be buyers had I watched, undisturbed? I pocketed a spoon and jumped back up into the vent.

Soon Billie made his way around the flat. I could hear him creeping about, and watched him tiptoe into the kitchen. He puffed up his chest and kept his fists up, like he was expecting Mike Tyson or something.

"Come out, or I'll kick the shit out of you!" He saw the drawers were open again. "Who's there? Come out, fuck nut!"

Ah, yes, that's precisely what I am. I dropped the spoon through the slats of the vent atop his head. He yelped and looked up, but could not see me. I could see him just fine, though—see the sweat on Billie's forehead, the whiteness of terror in his cheeks, the wide and shifting eyes. He'd never looked better.

Shakily, he bent down to pick up the spoon. He turned it in his palms, studying it as if it were the first time he had ever seen a bloody spoon. I wondered if he would see the watermarks or the tea stain he hadn't cleaned properly.

He put it back on the counter. Not back in the drawer. *The wrong way round.*

I punched the wall of the vent in fury, and he ran out, storming through the flat, checking every room, while I gave chase above him. He kept shouting, "Come out! Where are you! I will fucking kill you!" But I could see the fear in him. I could see the sweat and the way he jerked at every little sound.

I let the quiet swell, just to enjoy the waves of his terror. False security. He was not so easy to calm though; he circled back through the flat, turning on all the lights, even the bedside lamps, in the middle of the bloody day. He came out of his bedroom with a carving knife, eyes shifting at every shadow. That fucking knife. He knew how to keep *that* clean well enough, so why not the bloody spoons? The sight of how it glistened and gleamed like a god-damned diamond filled me with rage. But I held on to my temper, just about.

"This is some weird shit," he hissed. And then he whispered, "Is that you, Becca?"

Yep, definitely superstitious. "Becca? Becca, if you're here, I'm sorry for what happened to you. Becca, leave me alone. Please, just leave me alone!" he cried out, his knife held high.

While Billie crept into the bathroom and worked up the courage to pull back the curtain, I carefully gathered up the glass from the broken television and sprinkled it across the floor. He didn't wear his swanky trainers out in the rain, and he didn't wear them at home. Just when he wore them was still a mystery to me, but I didn't give a fuck.

He turned around in the bathroom just in time for the door to slam in his face. He tried to catch me in the act, but as soon as his bare feet crunched on the carpet he tripped up, crying out in pain. "Becca, you bitch!"

I hurried into the kitchen before he staggered in. I picked up a handful of spoons and scattered them on the counter, being sure to turn them the right way up. I placed a few end to end in a neat line, and arranged a second line beside it to match.

The kitchen door slammed open with a thud and Billie came hurtling into the kitchen, head soaked in sweat and chest heaving, knife raised like a fucking psycho. The first thing he noticed was my little spoon arrangement.

"Eleven," he muttered, confused. And then: "Eleven!"

I stepped forward and finally let him see me. When his face fell on me, it was priceless. Never seen a grown ass man look so terrified, like he could piss his pants on the spot. "Wait, please," he spluttered, dropping the knife and backing away.

I smiled at him, keeping my gaze firmly fixed on his as I bent to the floor. Now *I* had the knife, fuck nut. "It was eleven times, wasn't it?"

Old Jack

Jack's a bit of a tosser. Lives like the types you see in those budget horror flicks—house down some lost and forgotten track, often first seen by the camera shot sitting out on the deck or peeking behind a pair of nets that his gran put up in the thirties, sporting a dirty vest complete with holes. Jack is blissfully unaware of how fucking creepy he and his old house are, though; I doubt he's ever seen a horror film. I bet he just watches re-runs of *Carry On* films, slumped in a battered armchair, without once cracking a smile.

This isn't what makes Jack a tosser, though. You can't blame him for where he lives and for being too poor to buy a new vest. He's just fucking rude. I've been his postie for about a year because the last guy that delivered his sporadic mail straight up had a heart attack on his doorstep, and Jack didn't do shit. It was the boss who found Tommy the next morning, stiff as a board outside Jack's house. He'd gone round his route after Tommy's wife rang up to ask where the fuck he was, since he'd not come home and hadn't been seen at his local haunts. Jack said there wasn't anything he could have done, seen as he doesn't have a phone and can't walk far. He used to have to pick up his mail from the Post Office, he's so far off the beaten track; but he's got pretty bad arthritis, so the local GP persuaded us to go all the way down to his front fucking door. Jack never says thanks, and Jack never said sorry about Tommy. That's why Jack's a tosser.

He gets a small brown package once a week. No return address to say where it's come from. Wednesday, clockwork. It's light, square, flat. It's addressed to MR J. JACK on a small, printed label. Tommy asked him what the "J" stood for, back when he was the postie. We'd made bets down at the office about what it could be. James, Jacob, Josh, or straight up Jay. I bet on Jack, for a laugh. Jack Jack. Tommy came back with a massive grin on his fat face and told us what happened.

Tommy: "Hey Jack, what's the "J" for?"

Jack: [grumbled noises of confusion]

Tommy: "The "J"—on your post? Your first name."

Jack: "Jack."

I got fifty quid that day.

Before I was his postie, and before Tommy was his postie, Phil was Jack's postie. He'd asked him what was in the package one time, just being curious, but Jack wasn't happy about it. Went all red-faced, stammering around a cluster of swear words. Phil couldn't calm him down, and left old Jack standing on the porch, trembling like a fallen leaf trying to get back to the oak. Phil thought it would be a good idea to call the doctor and send him round, just to check on Jack. Turned out to be a bad idea for Phil: he got sacked. Broke the code of the postie. Don't ask, and don't peek. But fuck me, do I want to know what's in that little brown package. I want to know who gives a fuck about old

Jack the tosser who lives down the dirt track and doesn't do shit when a man ups and dies on his front fucking porch.

I'm pulling up to Jack's road now. You've got to park a bit off, because the road shrinks into a footpath. It's more like a trampled line through bushes, to be honest. There's wild flowers and nettles on either side, as high as my elbow. There's a light fall of rain which is kind of refreshing, I guess, but the breeze is a bit chilly as I step out of the van. Not much of a summer, as always. The walk is best in winter, when everything is dead and covered in frost. But the house looks that bit creepier when it's powdered with snow.

The roof's flat. The birds like nesting in the missing patches, in the shadow of the chimney. The smoke curls up and vanishes in the leaves of the trees surrounding the house all year round. It's always the first thing I see. After that comes the face of the house, toothless windows smiling under the frowning weight of the rusty drainpipes. I get to see all sorts of houses. One street could be full of back-to-backs, washing lines spider-webbing between the lot of them, screaming kids and barking dogs running about everywhere; the next is a long stretch of cottages, cobbled paths where horses clop, leading to gated entrances, perfect for one of those girly films set in the old days where everything is about marrying the rich bloke with a dirty secret. It's the same in this town as everywhere else, I guess. You get the extremes and you get the in-betweens looking up the ladder but shit scared of falling down a rung. But Jack's house, out here, out nowhere, a transplant of American horror in a little forgotten English town? It doesn't fit in. Jack doesn't fit in. I wish he had a dog or something. He wouldn't seem so damned weird if he did. Though I suppose the inside is full of those creepy stuffed dead animals with the dead glass eyes. So long as his dead mum isn't sat in a rocking chair too, I can live with that.

He's sat on the front steps chewing his tobacco, hunching forward. Looks like he's shaved recently, for a change; gone is the ragged fuzz that usually whiskers his cheeks, but stubble dots the skin of his chin in its stead. Yep, the vest's on, and the hole's bigger than I saw it last. I could see his pink nipple and the white hairs licking around it.

"Morning, Jack," I call out. Just because he's a tosser doesn't mean I have to be. "Weather's not bad today."

He grunts and takes the little package from my hand. I stand waiting for the thank you—just a habit, I guess. Of course, it didn't come. "Well. Bye, Jack."

I turn and saunter off. It's better walking away, with the house at your back, Jack out of sight, and only the high weeds and wild flowers with the bees floating about in front of you. Not quite a slice of Heaven, but a slice of—somewhere other.

"Can't see no sun from here."

I stop. Jack just fucking spoke. I turn to face him again. "What's that, mate?"

Jack spits a mouthful of tobacco on the ground at his feet. He sits for a moment, hands on his knees, looking me up and down as if he were only now seeing me for the first time, and not for every Wednesday of the last two and something years. He nods. I must've met his measure, or something. "Up there. Too many clouds." He points above his head.

The weather. He was talking about the fucking weather. Nothing more British than that; maybe he wasn't American after all. "Ah, yeah. Cloudy, isn't it? It's supposed to be sunnier tomorrow."

"Next Wednesday." He waves his package.

"Er, sure. See you next week."

When I get back to the office to clock out, I don't tell the gang about the conversation I'd had with Jack, for some reason. I wouldn't say it left me unsettled; nothing peculiar about a guy talking about the weather. But it was weird for Jack. I have this unexpected prize of words from the silent guy at the creepy house, words that should mean pretty much nothing but normal chit chat for passing strangers. *Can't see no sun from here.* I can't see no sun when I close my fucking eyes mate, but that's not exactly a conversation starter. I settle on reminding myself that Jack is Jack, and Jack is a tosser. Jack does weird things.

Rest of the week goes normal. All the normal houses with the normal people. I know most of their names, but they don't know mine. I know which houses have the friendly dogs and the ones with the dogs that savage the letters, which is fair enough, if you ask me, but I'd rather my fingertips weren't up for grabs at the same time. I know the houses that stink of weed, the ones that I have to half-near break the door down to be heard, the ones that will give me an eyeful when they open the door—nobody warns you about how many naked people you'll see as a postie, and it isn't an incentive to apply, I promise you.

Wednesday, again. There's a hum at the depot. Ever

gone to sleep on a summer afternoon with the window open and suddenly all the fucking blue bottles of the back garden buzz in? That's the kind of sound around the place. I get a few sideways looks and grins as I head to my locker. I pick up my bag and keys to the van, ready for the day, but that hum is in my head like a nesting insect. I go to the clerk's office, and find him shuffling dusty boxes about on the floor. Norman's one of those people who doesn't trust computers, and much prefers the filing cabinets with busted locks.

"What's the fuss about this morning?"

He blinks. "Nobody's told you?"

I shake my head.

He smiles at me. "Jack doesn't have his regular today. You can skip his house."

I smile back but I don't feel like smiling. I feel strangely deflated. I don't like going up to Jack's, nobody does. But this is out of routine. Jack will freak the fuck out. The GP visits him every Saturday afternoon, so by Monday I'm pretty sure we'll have a message from the Doc about Jack, asking us—me—to go down and explain why nobody came on Wednesday. If Jack had a phone, he could ask for himself, but of course he doesn't. He's some misplaced relic without the most basic communication skills.

Can't see no sun from here.

Fuck it. Fuck Jack. People's post goes missing all the time. Maybe the sender was caught short of a few bob and couldn't put the usual postage on it; could be delayed. If it arrived later today, it'll be sorted and sent out tomorrow, probably in Justine's bag. I bet Jack won't like her; I bet Jack hasn't seen a woman for fucking years. Justine definitely won't like Jack, or Jack's house. There'll be a shit storm tomorrow if she goes down there. Jack's got good aim with his tobacco spit. I've had a mouthful of it right on my shoe that one time when I was an hour later than normal.

I get in my van and sit there for a bit, thinking about it. Jack gets two visitors, the GP and me. And he gets a package. Not much for company. He's stuck in his gloomy American horror house in the suburb of a half-forgotten English village, sitting on the porch in a dirty vest, waiting for that package, whatever the fuck is in it. I can't even say it makes him happy, since I've never seen him smile. But he gets it, he takes it, it's old Jack's routine.

Fuck it. Not my responsibility. I turn on the ignition and head off. But by eleven o'clock, the time I'm usually heading toward Jack's place, I'm stuck thinking of the tosser again. It's hard to push him out of my head. There's nothing I can actually do about it. I deliver the post; I don't fucking make it. I couldn't even fake it if I wanted to—I've got no fucking clue what goes in there, and nobody dares ask after Phil got fired. I can't do anything, but I don't feel like doing nothing.

After I clock out at four p.m., I go home. I eat dinner, one of those micro meals from the co-op. I sit on the couch with the TV churning some shite, and I think. I can't stop. I get up and pour myself a glass of whiskey in the kitchen, and drink it in two bites—when it's a drink like whiskey, you make that grimace-y face and clench your teeth when it burns your throat, so you don't swallow it, you bite it down. I stand there, looking at my bottle like some noir detective, no crime to solve but the case of old Jack's missing package. It bugs me. I pour another glass but I stare at it instead of slinging it back. Jack is just stuck in my head.

So, stupid wanker that I am, I decide to head over to his house. Some Sherlock, though; it's only when I pull up that I realise I forgot my torch. I have to use the light on my mobile to follow the path. I stop when the shadow of the house looms ahead of me. The creepy fucking horror house. Yeah, I'm there. At night. To check on the psycho. Because he didn't get his weekly post.

Can't see no sun from here. Too right, mate.

I tread lightly on the steps to the porch, but of course they creak anyway. I go to the window instead of the door, just in case I can see old Jack happily chewing his tobacco on an armchair or whatever it is he might do alone at night. Part of the pane is broken, so it's easy to take a look—but there aren't any lights on in the front room, so there's only shadow to see. I can't hear anything but the night sounds and the wind in the trees, shaking the branches like a monkey on the hunt for nuts or something. Not an owl or a bat. Think of the decent animals that have fuck all to do with horror films.

I tap on the front door. I should've guessed it wouldn't even be locked. Jack hasn't got anything worth nicking and out here there aren't going to be any intruders—well, save me. I suddenly have this image of old Jack sleeping, snoring, wearing his grotty old vest on a dusty old bed, blissfully ignorant of my presence. In true American style, when he wakes up he'll whip a gun out from under his pillow and shoot me square between the eyes.

But. That was it—but. I need to know he's okay. Just because he's a tosser, doesn't mean I have to be. I walk right into the house and call out: "Jack? It's me." He doesn't know me from Adam, so that announcement isn't going to do any good. "Er—it's the postie. I wanted to check you're okay, because you didn't get your regular package. Jack? You okay?" I hear a moan, a proper ghostly wail. Just what I want to hear.

I walk carefully through the entrance and pass a couple of doors; the sounds are coming further back in the house. I'm not watched by any dead animals with dead glass eyes on the way through. Not even an impaled butterfly is stuck to the old walls. They're totally bare. Not one speck of old Jack is anywhere, not a puddle of tobacco. But I can hear him, moaning a deep and mournful sob. At least I think it's him. We've only recently exchanged words, so his sound is as new to me as the first cry of a baby.

It's coming from the last room on the right. A thin slice of orange light frames the door, the only shred of it in the whole damn place. Makes the dust on the floorboards glisten. I tap on the door. "Jack?" No reply.

I push the door open but linger behind it for a bit, just listening. If he's hurt himself, I've no fucking clue what to do. I can hardly remember why I even went there in the first place. But I am there, and Jack is upset or something, so I go in.

He's on the floor in the middle of the square little room, curled up. He looks frail; he must be nearer eighty than seventy, but I haven't really thought about it before. He's holding his head, crying into his arms. White tufts of hair escape the cracks between his rheumatic fingers. His legs are trembling—little fluttering kicks. Here is the butterfly, impaled by some mysterious grief about an undelivered package. Maybe a moth suits him better though, since he isn't much to look at it, and the orange lamp light is close beside him. It stretches his shadow into a thin and twisted darkness that melts into the wall. That shadow-Jack seems more real to me than the old man crying on the floor; the horror story is in the shadow, not in the man at my feet, and it's horror that I've been expecting.

I drop to my knees beside him. I put my hand on his shoulder, nice and light, so I don't startle him. "Jack? You're alright. Let me help you." He tries to form some words, but his sobbing is far too deep for me to understand. "Jack. I need you to move your hands away from your face so I can hear you." I wait a moment for him to move his arms by himself, but he just keeps talking, so I gently pull away an arm. "Jack?"

"There's no sun. There's no sun."

"I don't know what you mean, Jack."

He points ahead.

The wall opposite him is full of small square photos. Top to bottom, side to side. Piled on top of each other. I stand up, and draw nearer the wall to see what is in the photographs. The sun. They are all photographs of the sun. Nothing else. No tree, mountain, house, park, person, animal—nothing else in the camera shot but the sun in the sky. Some photos capture the sun escaping pursuant clouds; in others, the sun dips in from above, chasing the clouds away. In the photos on the right, the sun seems small and almost pink, while in the photos in the middle the sun is big and bright and fierce: full. I've never seen anything like it. In the low glow of the orange lamp, the sun seems to be setting in the room. More like, suns. The suns are setting, while old Jack cries.

"Is this—is this what you get each week, in the post?"

He isn't looking at me, and his arms are back over his head. He heaves in air. "The sun's gone."

I crouch beside him again. "No, Jack. It's still here, don't worry. It doesn't go anywhere; it just... hides for a bit. It's night."

He shakes his head. "No, no, no. The sun has gone. Wednesday. Wednesday, she sends the sun. She didn't. The sun has gone."

"What do you mean? Who sends the sun?"

He breaks down into more sobs. His whole body trembles. He doesn't say another word.

I have no choice but to ring the GP on his emergency number. I tell him where I am, what seems to be up with Jack. He tells me to leave him in the position he's in, keep talking to him and make sure he stays awake until he gets there. The Doc arrives about an hour later. He's all business, not asking any questions about the sun or the photos—he doesn't even seem to notice the wall. Maybe he's been in there before, I don't know. Nobody knows if anyone knows Jack at all. I kind of feel like I do.

I'm good for nothing other than that phone call—a phone call like Tommy had needed, but I didn't really feel like that made Jack a tosser anymore. Doc sends me away pretty quick, with a promise he can handle the situation, whatever the fuck's happening.

I don't sleep well when I get back. I don't know shit about why Jack is there, in that weird little room full of glass-sized suns in Polaroid squares; I don't know which "she" sent the suns, or why, or why she's stopped. Who would send an image of the sun? I don't know what any of it means. *Can't see no sun from here.* It hadn't seemed to bother him the other week, this supposed absence of sun; seemed like it was just a comment on the clouds. But in that creepy house he's made a temple out of the back room, a place where the sun is always in his sight.

Sleep doesn't happen, not a wink of it. Just old Jack in my head, crying. I'm that kind of tired that sticks in the eyes but keeps the heart pounding. Drink might help. With a sigh, I give up trying to sleep; it's only an hour before my alarm is due to shatter the silence anyway. I'm about to get dressed again, but then I remember I'd only taken my boots off to get into bed. I go down to the kitchen, bite down another shot of whiskey, straight from the bottle. It doesn't taste right. It isn't what I wanted.

So I leave my house, again. I get in the car and head off. Not to work—too early for that. I just drive for a bit, through the streets crowded with parked cars and out onto the widening avenues. The day is coming in slow, up ahead, orange splintering the blue dark, igniting the clouds pink, like blushing cheeks. For a moment my route loses the view of the sky, turning me back into the shadow of the silent streets as the road curves away; but it winds its way back, climbing up, breaking away from the houses until only a few old cottages appear.

The wind is more blustery up here, but the sky is... more. I don't come up here much; it's not on my route. But I've heard the kids call it "the top of the world". It's not really much of a hill, but you can look down onto the town from here and watch the blinking lights wake up at night. In the morning, though, it's more interesting to look up. The sun is here, big and bright and fierce: full.

I sit for a while, just watching, wondering at what point I should dig my sunglasses out of the glove compartment. I'm so deep in thought that I jump out of my skin when I hear the tap on the window. The Doc stands there, looking in. He has one of those faces that doesn't crack, not one bit—not for sorrow, not for joy, nothing. He gestures for me to wind the window down, to talk. So I do.

"As far as I can figure," he begins, looking pretty intently at me, "it's his sister. I used to think it was an old flame, but when I checked his birth certificate some years ago, I did some digging into his family medical history and found he has a sister. I think her name was Margot."

I blink. "What?"

"The one who sends the photos. I think it's his sister. She's eighty-four. I reckon she's died. I haven't told him that, though."

I nod. "I don't think you should."

"Well." He shrugs and scratches his head. "What do you think we should do?"

I get out of the car and take my mobile out of my pocket. I aim it, not quite square at the sun, but to catch a beam in the top right corner, so that the pink of the sky blushes below it, and glaze the photograph with a soft smile.

Acknowledgements

Cake Craft came to me quite unexpectedly during the first lockdown of Covid-19 in 2020. Living alone at a time when I could not see – could not embrace – loved ones led me to the inevitable: chocolate, treats, and writing. There seemed no better way to reconnect with my world than to write about it. So it would be remiss of me if I did not firstly thank the people in my life whose love and support have nurtured the person I am today, whose strength, compassion, and vivacity have inspired these pages.

I am eternally grateful to my parents for encouraging me throughout my creative journey since I first decided I wanted to be an author at 11. You were the first to know I'd decided the devil was an elderly dairy farmer from Yorkshire, and to read the opening. Thanks to my big sister, Lauren, who may not count reading as a hobby but happily reads my writing even so; thank you for encouraging my ambitions. I appreciate all of my family, for all of their cheerleading.

Thank you to my friends who have supported my ambitions. To Lauren, who read an early draft and reminded me of a few Yorkshireisms I should include. To Mim, who has read some parts of my other work in progress, and always cheers me on: I hope you enjoy *Cake Craft*, too! To Kelly, who always encourages me to love every part of myself. To Dil, who's been my best friend since school, and knows how much this means to me, and shares my excitement. To Fern, Edwin, and my burlesque buddies.

I'd also like to thank the teachers and lecturers who have nurtured my passion for learning, reading, and writing over many years: Amina, Ghislaine, Oz, and Rosemary. And, of course, the students I have had the pleasure of teaching, too.

Finally, I owe thanks to my publisher, Celine, for more than simply publishing my debut and guiding me through re-drafts and edits with support and enthusiasm. Our Friday afternoons as writing buddies during lockdown gave me a lot of comfort and helped me find joy while I was alone. I hope we can collaborate together in the future.

About the author

Hannah-Freya is a writer and academic based in West Yorkshire. Her PhD on horror and humour in the Gothic bleeds into her creative writing. She is fascinated by the blending of opposites – of elegance and vulgarity, of melancholy and wit. Her short story, 'Old Jack', won the Creative Showcase at Sheffield's Reimagining the Gothic in 2018. With Edwin Stockdale, a fellow academic, poet, and friend, she co-edited *Sleeping in Frozen Quiet*, a collection of poetry inspired by the Brontë family in association with the Leeds Centre for Victorian Studies at Leeds Trinity University. She is currently working on an epic fantasy affectionately known as "the sweary novel" among friends, which she sincerely hopes will be published in the near future. Writing updates and occasional witticisms can be found on her Twitter page @Freya_cw and Instagram @mentalwealthandhellbeing.

Ingram Content Group UK Ltd.
Milton Keynes UK
UKHW020804310523
422626UK00011B/275